Praise for Liz Matis

Playing For Keeps

RT Book Reviews: *Playing For Keeps* is entertaining ... an engaging storyline will keep readers turning the pages ... readers will enjoy the unfolding relationship and anticipate the sequel featuring the secondary characters.

Book Junkie: In Liz Matis' latest from Little Hondo Press, *Playing For Keeps* you will get a wildly sexy romance with depth and laughs. A page turner, bring on the sequel.

Love By Design

RT Book Review: Readers will get a kick out of these characters as they walk through a world of fashion and celebrities and soak up all the glitz and glam that a wild child and a bad boy could possibly provide.

Love on the Book Shelf: Don't hold this book too tight – you'll burn your fingers. Recommendation: Read this one if you need some warming up this winter. No joke. It's also the perfect just-before-bedtime reading, if you'd like some nice, sultry dreams.

ReRead: Totally worth it.

Going For It

Fantasy Football – Season 2

by
Liz Matis

And my lips are numb with such unbridled passion
Your naked shoulders reflect the shining of the night as I
contemplate the dance of my fingers
through your hair.

We love as there is not tomorrow
We love as lovers

I want to kiss even the shadow of your silhouette
in the street projects
And I want you to feel for a moment that you
belong to me.

Juan M. Frisanccio Muño

Chapter 1

Would he just leave already? Feigning sleep until Jake made his exit taxed Hannah's nerves and her resolve. Last night had been a mistake and she couldn't blame her poor judgment on alcohol nor from the romantic vibes surrounding Samantha's wedding day. Marriage was the furthest thing from Hannah's mind when she fell into bed with the best man.

Only dirty, hot sex had been on her mind—all day long—even during the church service.

Who thinks that way in church?

The devil had visited her right there at the altar. A sexy Satan in the solid form of Jake Miller standing confidently next to the groom as the vows were repeated, winking across the space to where she stood as the maid of honor. She had tried summoning the prayers of her youth in an effort to ward off the naughty feelings he evoked. Recalling the line, 'Now I lay me down to sleep', but that only led her thoughts further astray. What was wrong with her?

But it wasn't a matter of what was wrong with her, but what was so very right about Jake. Simply remembering his expertise in the bedroom caused her brain to take a vacation from all reason and for her soul to risk eternal damnation by lusting after him in a house of God. Her heart—encased in an iron box—was in no danger at all. Sealed shut with neither a lock nor a key for any man to search for. Fool was the man who did.

Hannah resisted the urge to stretch and ignored his not so subtle attempts to wake her up. Why couldn't he be a normal male—piss and get the hell out? But there was nothing normal about Jake. Nothing. Hannah's body still hummed with the proof. She smiled in her fake sleep.

"Dreaming of me?"

His rough voice, even sexier in the morning, washed over her as if she were bathing in a pool of ancient aphrodisiacs. How long had he'd been watching her? "No, of waffles."

His deep throaty laughter vibrated through her insides. Hannah was certain he could talk an orgasm out of her if he wanted to.

"I'll make you some. After…"

Jake pulled her close but she refused to nestle up against his warmth. "No need. I'm on a diet hence the dreaming of waffles. You may go."

Instead of complying he growled and rolled her onto her back using his weight to pin her to the mattress. His heavy erection pressed against the softness of her belly and she tried to squirm away but that only made his sex settle between her legs. His naughty chuckle annoyed and turned her on all at the same time. She raised her chin in defiance. But she wasn't going anywhere. Built like the football player he was, his physical strength sent a rush of liquid desire through her body. Now, she didn't want him to go.

"Listen up Hannah. I'm not one of your boy toys who you can play hot and cold with."

She started to deny it but the look in his eyes stopped her.

"And if you try it again I'll make you so hot for me you'll have to beg for it." Those full lips crushed her mouth in a smoking kiss that left no doubt in her mind that he could do just that.

Hannah stroked the smoothness of his bald head, wondering what he would look like with hair. But Jake Miller was so damn sexy without long locks that she imagined there were men who shaved their heads to emulate the Cougars flashy running back.

Damn Samantha and Ryan for getting married. Hannah had become an expert in avoiding Jake and now she wanted to chain him to her bed and never let him leave despite the fact that only minutes ago she claimed to have wanted him gone. She didn't want him as a boy toy—she wanted to enslave him. But it was he who was enslaving her. With his kiss and his touch and oh...

"You're in my blood, Hannah, but don't expect me to bleed for you." With that, he flipped off the bed and pulled on white boxer briefs.

His yummy caramel skin begged to be licked like a candy apple and like a spoiled child denied a treat Hannah whined. "But what about?" She pointed to the erection straining against the fabric of his briefs.

"I think I made my point."

"But..."

Jake walked back to the bed. "Don't make the mistake of thinking I'm ruled by this." He took her hand and rubbed his cock with it, biting his lip and tilting his head to the side like he was trying, but failing to prove his statement. He raised her hand to his heart. "Or by this."

But Hannah thought that had to be a lie. The beat beneath her palm, rapid and unsteady, matched her own.

"Not even here." He quickly tapped his bald head then slid her fingers down to his cut abs. "I go with my gut."

Her nails dug into his chiseled flesh, not an ounce of fat on him. He could easily land an endorsement deal for men's underwear. No stuffing required. "And what does your gut tell you?"

Backing away, he grabbed the rest of his clothes, flipped them over his shoulder, and left the room without a word.

"Good. I wanted you to leave in the first place," she huffed.

"I'm going to make us waffles," he yelled from the hallway. "My gut is hungry and you look hungrier."

Hannah grabbed the pink silk robe hanging from the four-poster bed and followed him into the kitchen as she slid it on. "I have a shoot within two days. I can NOT eat waffles."

He ignored her, grabbing the waffle iron and plugging it in. He hummed a tune as he raided the fridge and mixed up the batter with strong, steady strokes. Jake looked at home in her kitchen like he'd only been gone a weekend and not months, which again annoyed and charmed her all at the same time. Even though he was unshaven and shirtless, he almost seemed domesticated but Hannah knew better. Men like Jake could not be tamed. It was better to return them to the wild before you became attached. It was a lesson she'd wished her Mother had learned.

Did he just sprinkle nutmeg in the batter? Her mouth watered.

As he poured the batter into the waffle maker he stopped humming and asked, "What I don't get is that we had this big blow-out about you doing Playboy—you break up with me over it—and then you don't do it. Why?" He looked at her with a penetrating gaze.

His light brown eyes reminded her of the wolf she'd admired at the Central Park Zoo. Jake forbid Hannah to pose and nobody tells her what to do so she told him to take his archaic views of women and shove it up his ass. Until last night they hadn't seen nor spoken to each other in seven long sex deprived months. At least she'd been sex deprived. She'd bet Jake lasted all of a day before he moved on. "Well, it wasn't because of you."

"Then why not do it?" He took the pants he'd thrown onto the chair and pulled them on.

"You are so full of yourself." She gave a snarky laugh. "Victoria Secret gave me another year on my contract. I negotiated to be on the cover of the swimsuit issue. Which is a miracle, aging model that I am."

"Aging? Hannah you're barely into your thirties."

Thirty-one, to be exact. Hannah shuddered at the number. She was ancient compared to the hot slutty girls of today though she supposed that's what the supermodels of the late nineties thought about her when she burst onto the scene. "I'm a dinosaur."

Jake zipped up. "You're more beautiful today."

Hannah huffed in disbelief.

He approached her with a gleam in his eye and pulled the bow that held her robe together and slid his hands up the swell of her hips. "You were the girl next door, but now you're a beautiful female fatale with curves."

"Fat." She pushed him away. In the real world she wasn't but in the fashion world? She was a horse. But Victoria Secret liked curvy models and she was more likely to be fired for being too skinny than for gaining a couple of pounds.

"Really Hannah?

She looked away remembering the latest designer who pinched at her waist and told her she was thickening. Thickening!

"Your body would drive any man insane. Believe me, I know. I'm one step away from Bellevue."

"Hmm, so says the man who left me high and dry not five minutes ago."

Anger flashed in his eyes. "Is that what you want—a lap dog to do your bidding?" He lifted her up onto the counter and pushed himself between her legs. "Or a man who knows what you want? What you need. And will give it to you."

He kissed her with a hungry thirst, like a vampire ravenous for blood. Hannah reveled in her feminine power as he lost control. She felt exactly like the female fatale he'd claimed her to be. She'd won. He'd take her right there, right now. No man could resist her. Then the waffle iron dinged. Jake stopped and stepped back before she could tightly wrap her legs around his torso.

"Enjoy the waffles." He lifted the handle of the iron and grabbed his shirt and pulled it on.

"You're leaving?" she nearly shrieked the question. Hannah couldn't believe it. Her body pulsed with want. With need. How could he do this to her?

"That's what you've wanted ever since you woke up this morning."

She couldn't stop the frown she knew was forming on her face. *Great, now I'm risking damn wrinkles over this man!*

"Your move, Hannah."

She meant to say something clever, to regain some sort of dignity, but the door had already shut. Just as well. How dignified could she be sitting on the kitchen counter, her robe and legs wide open with steam from that damn appliance spouting into the air?

And damn him if those waffles didn't smell really, really good.

Chapter 2

J ake flagged a cab outside Hannah's posh Eastside address. Only after climbing in and giving the driver his downtown one did he allow himself to fume. You'd think she'd be happy he hadn't rushed out the door like a gigolo or that he wasn't a pig who got off on seeing his girlfriend naked in a magazine and brag about it to his friends.

It was bad enough his teammates had posted pictures of Hannah from the Victoria Secret catalog all around the locker room to taunt him. To remind him of what he lost when she dumped him.

But last night he'd won her back.

Now he had to figure out how to turn this into a winning streak. The long months apart from Hannah had him questioning everything from his manhood to his sanity. He tried calling her at first, but when she didn't return his calls his pride demanded he play it cool. Still, that didn't mean he hadn't listened intently to every word Samantha said in case she let some vital piece of information slip or relieved when Ryan would throw him a bone with the simple statement of 'She's not dating anyone.' Then Jake would act like he didn't care and even though his teammate knew the score he'd let Jake slide.

The gossip pages, where Hannah often appeared, offered nothing. But that didn't mean she wasn't sharing another man's bed.

The not knowing was torture.

For a while he tried pretending she didn't exist—that her loveliness was a figment of his imagination, but her soft moans along with her fevered pitch screams of his name haunted his dreams. Hannah was so right—he did dream of her.

So when he saw the deep rose color of the bridesmaid dress, the memory of the lingerie she wore that first night they made love lingered throughout the day. Jake wondered if she chose the color on purpose to torment him. During the ceremony he undressed her inside his wicked mind— the dress falling to the floor unveiling the bra and panties underneath and then down to nothing but the natural rose-colored areas of her banging body. God worked a true masterpiece when he created Hannah. Before he left he should've asked the priest for an emergency Confessional. Hell, when it came to Hannah he'd need a priest on speed dial to keep up with his sinful thoughts and deeds.

One thing was for certain she didn't have to worry about re-purposing the dress, as it now lay shredded on the bedroom floor. His deep satisfied smile reflected off the window of the cab.

Yes, he won last night and this morning, but what next? Hannah tossed men to the side like they were her playthings she'd gotten bored with. She needed a strong man to call her on her crap.

She was used to men giving her anything she wanted but they never gave her what she needed. Jake could, if she'd let him.

Granted he mishandled her initial decision to pose nude. In the end she declined the offer and even though she said it had nothing to do with him, she lied. It had everything to do with him and his belief that she wasn't a plaything.

What was up with models anyway? Jake dated quite a few and all of them were insecure behind the glitz and glamour. Paid to be pretty, models should be the most confident of women. He didn't get it.

But he wanted to get Hannah because there was something so vulnerable about her that grabbed at his heart. Her smile could bring him to his knees faster than a three hundred pound tackle.

With eyes as big and blue as the Texas sky where he played college ball and long hair that swayed like the amber waves of grain, Hannah embodied the traits of the Midwestern beauties that won Miss U.S.A. pageants, but with the Jersey girl attitude that was her birthright.

Last night he'd beat out twenty of his teammates for the bride's garter and the right to slip it onto the maid of honor's long sleek leg. For a moment he felt like Prince Charming but then Hannah ruined the fantasy by ordering him to get it over with it and he turned into the Big Bad Wolf and rode that garter all the way up the stairway to Heaven and brushed her sex with his finger. It wasn't over. Not by a long shot.

But where did he go from here? Just show up at her doorstep tonight? Ask her out on a date? No, not after telling Hannah it was her move.

His cell rang with the ringtone to Roy Orbison's *Pretty Woman* and he laughed wondering when she had the chance to download it. "Miss me already?"

"Hardly. My vibrator will take care of what you didn't."

"Go for it. We never did finish that phone sex experiment."

He heard a frustrated sigh at the other end. Last time they tried it he ended up at her apartment for the real thing.

"I think that experiment was very successful." Hannah finally said.

Jake laughed. "Remember that when the batteries die."

"Hey, you're the one who left."

"Point taken. Now, what's up?"

"I have a charity dinner to go to tonight and I was wondering…wondering…"

Jake let her stutter, he was a most patient man.

"…if you would escort me?" The words rushed out of her mouth.

Jake could feel the grin widening on his face. "Hannah, are you asking me out on a date?" he asked slyly.

"Noooo. No. Like I said—escort."

He pictured her checking out her flawless manicure as she said it. And while he loved when those blood red nails scratched and dug into his back when she came he knew he had to be strong. "Escort? Sorry the name does not fit the man."

"Oh, and you don't consider me a trophy girlfriend?"

"Girlfriend." Jake considered the term for a moment. "Now that's more like it. But trophy?" He gazed out the window thinking of all his past accolades and felt the weight of the Super Bowl ring on his finger "I've got plenty of trophies. None of them keep me warm at night." He lowered his voice on purpose knowing Hannah would cave.

"Fine, it's a date thingy then."

"Great, pick you up at 7:00."

"7:15."

Jake wore down her defenses and he'd gained a lot of yards on this play so he'd let her have this. "Be ready."

Chapter 3

Hannah meditated as Brooke, make-up artist extraordinaire, put the finishing touches onto the face People Magazine named to their most beautiful list. Without the special effects like airbrushing, and the proper lighting she could be the girl next door. The reality of what it took to create an image that women aspired to be amounted to a magic show. Hannah never left the house with what she called her 'face'. She'd never get caught on one those Stars Without Makeup pages. Jake had been the only man ever to see her sans make-up. To his credit, he didn't even seem to notice and would ravage her in the morning light. Except this morning, of course, but she knew he was trying to prove a point. That she wanted him.

Nerves tightened inside her stomach. The man always set her on edge. Of course it could just be hunger pangs. Yes, that's all it was.

The doorbell rang, and she pictured her assistant Nate, dressed in black skinny jeans and a neon green blazer, answering the door and then Jake impatiently glancing at his watch, upset that he had to kill time in her living room, especially after ordering her to be ready. He'd wait and he won't complain one bit. Not once he laid eyes on her. She was pulling out all the stops.

"All done."

Hannah peered into the adeptly named vanity mirror. "You're truly an artist, Brooke. In every sense of the title Make-up Artist."

"Please, you're not a challenge."

"I barely look like I'm wearing any."

Brooke was a beauty in her own right but was several inches shorter than the average model. "Well, yes that is the trick."

"See? Genius. The Leonardo Da Vinci of the make-up world."

"Hmmm, maybe I should put that on my business card," said Brooke as she packed up her case filled with the tools of the trade.

Nate opened the door and poked his head in. "He's pacing. He reminds me of a Latino Rhett Butler."

Hannah shook her head. "What? He's bald. No moustache. And I don't think he's even Latino." Jake's light caramel color starkly contrasted with Hannah's almost ghost like skin. A fleeting picture of what their children would look like faded before it could fully form.

"Whatever. He's yummy all the same. Besides it's all in the attitude." Nate snapped his fingers.

Brooke closed up her case. "Oh, I have to check him out before I leave." She rushed out of the bedroom as Nate entered.

"You know if you're going to keep this one you should think about changing the décor of your boudoir." Nate helped her with the clasp of a pink diamond necklace.

Hannah glanced around the room and noted the frilly lace pillows, pink walls, and sparkly chandelier. "Who said I'm keeping him?" Walking over to the huge full-length mirror propped up against the wall she added, "Besides, if you ask him what color my walls are he wouldn't be able to tell you."

Nate came to stand beside her. "You look like a life-sized Barbie doll," said Nate.

"And in my living room is my so-not-like-Ken doll."

"Thank God. Ken is not anatomically correct."

A naughty smiled appeared on Hannah's face. "Jake is beyond correct."

"Don't make me hate you, girl," said Nate with dramatic flair.

"Hannah!" bellowed Jake from the living room.

"I wouldn't keep him waiting any longer. He'll come in here and get you himself."

Hannah laughed. "Can't let him ruin my grand entrance." She twirled out of the room pretending she was in the middle of a fairy tale. As long as she didn't expect a happy ever after at the end she could pretend all she wanted.

"Your lat—"

Hannah performed her Red Carpet pose. The overhead lights danced off the sparkles of the deep pink dress. "You were saying?"

Jake slowly approached her—no, not so much as approached as in stalked. He reached out and curled a tendril escaping the upswept ponytail around his thick finger and rubbed the texture with his thumb. Then he stepped in closer. Hannah couldn't speak, couldn't move. He had frozen his prey and all he had to do was go in for the kill.

"You're the beauty to my beast, Hannah."

A thrill shot up her body and settled in her chest making it hard to breathe. Jake may act like a caveman from time to time, and though he sported an Armani black tuxedo with a dark, gray silk shirt he still looked like a bad boy, but he was no beast. He only proved her right when he unwound the strands and caressed her cheek as if she were a delicate orchid.

She leaned into the caress for a moment, savoring his touch on her skin, scared to tell him she thought he was gorgeous and sexy but then opened her eyes and bravely admitted, "You're handsome."

Jake's tongue slid along his lips like a wolf ready to devour it's prey. "I'm glad you think so, but I was referring to how I'm feeling on the inside."

Under the influence of his low, sultry voice, Hannah's knees buckled and she thought she might actually swoon. Now she understood Nate's Rhett Butler comparison. *Get a grip. This isn't some 20th century romance novel. I just need to breathe.* Or perhaps it was those hunger pangs causing her to feel faint.

"Baby doll, if you don't stop staring at me like I'm your next meal I won't be responsible for another torn gown."

"Sounds like I'm going to need a leash."

Jake shook his head no. "You're going to need chains."

Chains? But all he needed to enslave her was his words.

He brushed a light kiss across her frosted lipstick. "Hell, maybe even a whip."

His kiss deepened and so did her growing need. He was probably ruining all of Brooke's hard work but Hannah didn't care. Make-up could be re-touched. If only the heart could be so easily mended then maybe she'd risk loving Jake.

"Seriously Hannah, you're going to have to be the strong one here or we'll never leave," he said in a thick whisper.

Fueled with feminine power, Hannah stepped back and pulled him to the door, adding a sashay in her step and laughed when Jake practically grunted.

Once settled in the limo she asked him if he wanted champagne, which he declined with a shake of his head. "I'm a scotch man."

Hannah sipped from the flute since she didn't know what to say. They never really talked before. Their past relationship—if you can call a one-week affair a relationship—had been solely based on sex. The one time they talked seriously was the one time they argued and then promptly broke up. Jake fiddled with his tie and she supposed he struggled with the right words as well. If only their minds connected as well as their bodies joined together. "I wonder what Samantha and Ryan are doing," she ventured.

"What I'd rather be doing to you right now."

"Oh." His words conjured visions of last night. Of his hands sliding possessively over her body. Of his mouth claiming hers. Of him entering her gently. It hadn't felt like sex. Well, the second time hadn't. The first time—oh yeah, definitely hot and raw sex.

Silence descended again and so did Hannah's nerves. Maybe she was kidding herself. Just because Jake triggered explosive orgasms deep within the well of her being didn't mean anything other than that he had a lot of practice. Once football season started he'd probably go back to his low-maintenance, groupie bimbos. *Stop thinking! Talk. Say anything. Just stop thinking!*

"Nate thought you were Latino," she blurted.

"Did he?"

"Yeah. So I was wondering—"

"Does it matter?"

Hurt filled her heart. "Well, no, obviously it doesn't. I was just making conversation." She wouldn't admit it to him now but she was trying to get to know him. Other than his occupation, gift for making women melt and mixing up a batch of waffles that would make any woman sigh, Hannah knew nothing about him. And he brushed off her first attempt to reach out to him. Obviously she was a trophy. *Just shut up and look pretty Hannah.* She looked out the window before Jake could see the tears welling up.

"Hey, Hannah. Don't get mad. Growing up I put up with a lot of shit. Didn't know where I belonged. Even within my own family." Jake reached out and tilted her face back to his. "I didn't want to think it made a difference to you."

"I didn't mean to pry."

"Are those tears?"

"No."

Jake didn't call her on the lie, merely brushed away a lone drop with his thumb. "I'm quarter Black, quarter Italian, and the other half so mixed up I make a mutt out of the pound look like a candidate for the Westminster Dog Show," he said adding a laugh.

But Hannah didn't find it funny. "You're exotic. Perfect." How could anyone think otherwise?

"Men can't be exotic. Now what about you Miss American Pie?"

"Hardly. My father's side is from Russia. I even speak Russian." Hopefully, he wouldn't ask about her mother, who was from the former white ruling class of South Africa when she immigrated to the States. He'd think that his racial background did matter and it didn't to her. Her mother? That was a different story.

"Really?"

"I can do more than pose, you know." Annoyance lit her voice. She was tired of everyone thinking she was a dumb blonde.

"I'm aware of that."

"In fact, I speak Spanish fluently and can converse in Japanese." Hannah had an ear for languages that she discovered while on modeling assignments around the world. And boy oh boy she was big in Japan where she'd done several commercials.

"Impressive. Say something in Russian for me." Jake took her hand and interlocked their fingers.

The connection reminded her of last night, of their long limbs entwining until it seemed as if they were one person. Her heart leapt as if it were trying to escape the box she sealed it away in. She feared Jake had solved the riddle to open it. So she said to him what she couldn't say in English. "Я падаю для вас," she said with her best Russian accent.

"That is so sexy. What does it mean?"

I'm falling for you. Hannah wasn't about to reveal the true meaning of the words. "It means I want to sit on your face."

Jake's deep laughter filled the confined space. "Later," he promised. The limo pulled up to the Red Carpet. "Do you think we'll land one of those smashed up names like Bradgalina?" he grimaced.

Hannah blinked and her stomach dropped. It'd been a long time since she'd been romantically linked with a man and it seemed like Jake wasn't relishing his upcoming role either. The media circus was about to begin. Shaking off the dread, she reached for her phone, deciding to beat the paparazzi at their own game. "Wait Jake." She waved the phone in the air. He put his arm around her, their heads touched as she held the phone out. With his musky cologne lighting up her erogenous zones it was hard to concentrate on posing. She snapped the photo and then retrieved the picture to view it. It passed inspection and she tweeted it to the world.

"How many followers do you have?"

"Something like 2 million."

"Most of them men, I bet," said Jake as he got out of the limo and held out his hand.

Hannah didn't know if that was a rhetorical question or not and besides she didn't know the answer. Tweeting about makeup tips and dating advice she doubted Jake's assumption. She placed her hand in his and slid out carefully so that the slit on her dress didn't expose the lace panty thong she wore underneath.

The flashing lights blinded her for a moment as the paparazzi rushed to get a shot of the new couple. Still holding her hand, they walked a few feet until the shouts of the photographers forced them to stop for another photo. Then like any good escort on the red carpet, Jake stepped aside to allow Hannah to be photographed alone. Even though he was within arms reach she missed him being right by her side. A camera crew and interviewer stepped up to Jake. "Jake Miller, Super Bowl MVP with Supermodel Hannah Hahn! How long has this been going on?"

Hannah pretended to ignore the question as she held her smile but did side step a bit closer to listen to Jake's response as the interviewer held out the microphone.

"I loved Hannah from afar for a long time."

Oh he was good.

"Tell us what's your favorite part of Hannah's body?" the interviewer asked in a tone better suited to conspirators.

Hannah's mouth dropped slightly but she quickly recovered hoping no one caught it on camera. She turned to glance at Jake and caught his annoyed gaze before he slowly took in her form.

"Hmmm, so much to choose from."

She blushed and looked away to finish up with the photographers.

"But I have to say it's her heart."

Her heart? Her eyes bugged out. Oh my God that was going to be an unattractive photo. And of course that would be the one to hit the papers. How she kept a smile plastered to her face as Jake continued to praise her work with the Wounded Warriors Project could only be attributed to her many years in front of the camera.

How did he know? She didn't get a chance to tell Jake. In fact, she never spoke about her charity work to anyone unless she was running an event like tonight.

Her heart? Not her boobs, or legs. Nor any of the other various parts of her body that sold products to millions of women. *My heart.* Finished with posing Hannah turned away from the paparazzi and as Jake took a step closer so did she and before she knew what she was doing, planted a big kiss on his lips.

Chapter 4

The heat of the flashbulbs was nothing compared to the scorch of Hannah's lips. He lied when he said his favorite body part was her heart. Not that Hannah, try as she might to hide her tender side, didn't have a huge heart behind the voluptuous breasts that spilled out of the Victoria Secret bras she modeled. If he were being truthful, he would've said her pouting lips shaped like a bow drove him wild.

But he wasn't about to tell that ass of an interviewer whose sexist question objectified Hannah as a plaything. Perhaps this explained her fixation on her looks.

By her unbridled response he'd say he won some brownie points with his answers. Though he hoped she didn't read anything into his statement that he loved her from a far. Women, he knew, could make up a whole story from one innocent sentence.

The kiss ended as spontaneously as it began and he told himself it was the flash of the cameras that stunned him and not the luscious lips breaking away from his. But as she stepped back he believed for a moment that the smile on her face was for him alone and not for the paparazzi. The bluest of eyes shone back at him like he was her whole world. It seemed women weren't the only ones who could make up a story. *Back to reality Jake.*

She tugged on his sleeve to move inside. The simple gesture pulled at his heart and he reminded himself how easily she tossed him aside after the silliest of arguments. He barely survived it and they had only been together for a week. He'd planned to walk away after last night even if it meant alienating his best friend's new wife. But like a recovering addict presented with his first temptation after a long stint in rehab, he relapsed.

Jake believed a good offense was a good defense, so while he foolishly planned to see this to the final play, he'd re-evaluate his game plan and shore up the blocks around his heart. Big, badass running back brought down low by a mere kiss.

He followed Hannah's lead into the ballroom keeping his hand splayed across the small of her back. A gesture more to center them in the sea of celebrities piling in like it was the Academy Awards, than an act of possession.

Hannah had a lot of pull, though a celebrity would be committing career suicide by turning down an invite to a Wounded Warriors Project fundraiser. Once inside she turned to him. "Um, I do have to mingle. Do you want to make the rounds with me?"

"You go ahead." Jake had no desire to be introduced as Hannah's latest. "I see some of the guys."

"Okay." Hannah shrugged.

"Unless you want me to?" In front of the world Hannah appeared confident but when they were alone she let down her guard and he could feel the uncertainty radiating from her.

"No. Go have a good time."

He approached his teammates who were more comfortable in a group than working the room.

"Twenty-four hours and she hasn't dumped you yet," said Glock, the other running back who gunned for Jake's starting role each year.

The muscle in Jake's jaw twitched and he quickly smiled so not to let on how much the dig hurt.

"So are they real?" asked Todd, the quarterback. "You never did tell us."

Usually he'd answer with a crude remark. Hell, he'd offer up information. But Hannah was different. Hell, he was different when he was with her. Saying things he would never say, feeling things he'd never felt.

"Can't understand why she's with you," jibed Glock. "It's not like she needs your money."

"I bet she rakes in more than you," said Todd.

That did not bother him. He hated gold diggers who were the worst kind of woman. After a knee injury sidelined him during his junior year in college his girlfriend of two years went after a more profitable target, his team's quarterback. During the long rehab back into playing shape he vowed he'd never let another woman get under his skin. It was a vow he kept until Hannah embedded herself into every pore of his being.

But if she wasn't after his money then what was she after? Despite her humble upbringing she fit right in with the high society crowd that saw him as an uncouth thug. They would assume he coasted on classes like basket weaving instead of earning dual degrees in Pre-Law and Business Administration.

When his body was used up and his playing days were over so were the parties and fame. And the women. So many women. Man, he was a pig. And a hypocrite for thinking the interviewer was an ass.

Despite the fact that football and modeling were as different as winning and losing, both were businesses that considered the both of them commodities, chattel even. Hannah gains a couple of pounds and she loses modeling assignments. He gets a concussion and he's expected to play. Both of their careers have shortened life spans. At thirty-two he was considered a veteran.

Maybe that's why Ryan settled down, to ease his way into retirement after the upcoming season. Ryan had taken one too many hits to the head but Jake felt stronger than ever and had a couple of good years left. Still, he wondered if he was the settling kind. Was Hannah? Did she want kids?

She had him wanting answers to questions he'd never thought he'd be asking.

From this vantage point he could see Burner, the second-year tight-end slide up to Hannah. "Catch up with you guys later."

"Miller don't hurt him too bad," called out Todd.

"Ask if she'll introduced me to any of her Angel friends," yelled Glock.

Jake rounded the edges of the ballroom, using the time to calm his boiling emotions to a simmer. He came to stand behind a panel and what he overheard Burner say ignited a firestorm of possessive feelings inside him. He refused to call it jealousy.

"Miller's washed up. An old man."

"He's the Super Bowl MVP. And you're just a boy."

He'd feel bad for the kid if he weren't sniffing around Hannah. Jake stepped from around the panel. "Burner, thanks for keeping my woman amused."

"Oh, was he trying to be funny? I thought he was just delusional."

Hannah's supermodel bitch act was in full mode. Happy it was not directed at him he could afford to be cool. "Man, you better get out of here while she's being nice."

Burner adjusted his jacket like Hannah's put down hadn't put a dent in his huge ego and left.

Hannah turned to him, narrowing her eyes. "My woman?"

"Take it easy. Just making it clear to the kid so he doesn't get confused in the future."

"Great," Hannah gestured quotation marks with her fingers as she continued with, "teammate" you got there."

Jake shrugged his shoulders like it didn't bother him. "You did invite him." Now *that* bothered him.

"I invited the whole team."

"Except me."

Hannah's pout almost undid him. "Now Jake." Her fingers trailed up the lapel of his jacket. "I didn't ask you because I wouldn't have been able to bear it if you came with a date."

"So you understand how I feel when I see you with another man?"

"I do." Hannah conceded. "And I'm not beyond starting a cat fight."

There wasn't a man on the planet, civilized or not, who wouldn't pay good money to see that, especially if the fight was over themselves. "Let's dance."

"I really should get back."

"Just one." He couldn't wait to get her in his arms and stake his claim before any of the other men got ideas of coming on to her. Because while two girls going at it was hotter than hell, he'd likely kill his opponent. As they approached the dance floor she pulled away. "What's the matter?"

"Let's wait for something slower."

"Come on, a little Salsa never hurt anybody."

"If you're talking about the stuff you put on tacos I would agree but the dance? I might maim you with these heels."

Jake laughed. "Those heels do look lethal."

Hannah pointed to a woman shaking her business. "I can't move like that."

He leaned in, increasing the pressure of his hand on the naked curve of her back, propelling her forward. "With the way you move in bed I find that hard to believe," he whispered into her ear, adding a rush of air. Her shiver warmed him all over.

When they reached the center of the dance floor, he said, "Just follow me." They took a few tentative steps, but despite the sultry beat of the music her body locked up into a mannequin pose, even her smile was tight. "Loosen up a little."

If anything she froze up more. "I think my first time went a little like this."

"Yeah, but I know what I'm doing."

Her body visibly relaxed and a blush tinged her cheeks and he caught a glimpse of the virginal teenage girl she used to be. His throat constricted, making it hard to swallow, his heart contracted in his chest making it difficult to breathe, and Jake thought when it came to Hannah he didn't know what he was doing at all.

Chapter 5

Those words 'loosen up a little' haunted Hannah for sixteen years. But Jake's gentle and encouraging smile swept the horrible memories back into the hidden corners of her mind.

She weakened all over when he whispered into her ear, enticing her to move to the pulsating rhythm. With his hands on her hips she easily danced in sync with him.

"Good," mouthed Jake as he backed away, sliding his hands back into the partner dance hold.

She panicked for a moment hoping she didn't look like an idiot but if you were going be an epic fail you should at least do it with style. Calling on her supermodel persona, power surged through her body. If she could rock the runway to any beat thrown at her while wearing a bra, panties, and a pair of giant angel wings attached to her back—she could do this.

"That's it. I knew you'd be a natural."

He wouldn't say that if he knew about her disaster of an 8th grade dance. Tall, gangly, and new to the school, not even her years on the pageant circuit could save her from the awkwardness of being five inches taller than any boy there. The one boy who did ask her to dance soon regretted it and laughed at her clumsy movements, sending her running to the bathroom in tears. It was Samantha who helped to dry those tears, consoling Hannah with these words of wisdom. "His sister told me he pees in his bed."

Still, she'd never danced to anything but unhurried, melodic love songs.

"I think you're ready for a twirl," shouted Jake over the music.

Hannah didn't have time to shake her head as she spun for a split second, then fell right back into step. Wow, he was good. She practically didn't have to do anything. Fearing a wardrobe malfunction, she glanced down at her gown. When she took a misstep Jake smoothly turned it into a dip. He'd be a perfect celebrity for *Dancing With The Stars*.

Laughing as he pulled her upright, she finally gave into the music and to Jake. He was right; he knew exactly what he was doing.

And not just when it came to dancing.

The sex alone would keep her coming back for more. But it ran deeper than that. Jake knew how to make her feel special. She sensed he wasn't with her because she was Hannah Hahn, Supermodel but because she was just Hannah. Unlike other men she dated he didn't survey the room internally saying, 'Look who I'm with.'

She could be herself around Jake. He made her believe that was enough.

Even though she was in great shape from running half marathons on the treadmill and pumping on the elliptical like a mad woman, Hannah was gasping for breath by the end of the song. Perhaps the pounding of her heart came from being in his arms, of his smiling at her like she was the only woman in the room—in the world. "Thanks. That was fun." They walked off the dance floor holding hands. "I better get back to my hosting duties."

"Sure."

Hannah turned to go but Jake held onto her hand and her eyes met his amused gaze. "Save the last dance for me."

It should've sounded corny. But that voice, sincere and deep, made it anything but. And she knew the last song of any party would be a mood setter for the night to come.

On the ride back to her apartment Jake playfully tugged on her ponytail like he was a grade school boy and she giggled in return. The conversation flowed back and forth, the complete opposite of the drive to the event. Was it dancing together that created this sense of closeness that not even great sex the night before had been able to achieve?

Now his whispers spoke to her heart, a simple touch sent her skin afire, and a knowing look peered into her soul. An unopened bottle of champagne chilled in the limo fridge, but Hannah had no need of it. Bubbles of excitement coursed through her blood creating a buzz inside her head. That wasn't the only place buzzing. She rubbed her legs together to ease the ache between her thighs.

Jake took note of the movement, his hand riding up her leg as he whispered. "Are you already wet for me, Hannah?"

Her breath caught. Why did Jake's dirty talk make her throb with wickedness? Was it the complex bass tone mixed with a slight Texan inflection or the edge in his voice as if he was at the end of his limits and ready to jump into the abyss with her? Or was it because she knew on the other side she'd be clean and whole. "Why don't you find out for yourself?" She reached over to raise the privacy panel but then the limo pulled up to her building. A disappointed sigh escaped her mouth.

"Just as well." Jake inched his hand back down her leg. "What I have in mind for you can't be rushed."

What did that mean? Sounded like torture and not the glorious rush of release she needed. Right. Now.

Jake didn't touch her as they walked in the building and rode up the elevator. Didn't speak. Was he playing some sort of game? Entering the apartment she tossed the keys on the entry side table and though she wanted to throw herself at him, she decided to beat him at his own game and asked in a calm voice, "Do you want a drink?" She would not be the mouse to his cat.

"What I want is to tear that slip of fabric away from your body and leave you naked for the rest of eternity."

Oh, not a cat at all, but a Cougar like his team's namesake. She followed him to the bedroom like a harem girl following her Sultan. This was so unlike her. In and out of bed she controlled a relationship not the other way around.

He walked over to the full-length mirror loosening his tie. Why wasn't he making a move? Maybe this is where she could take the control back. Push him into bed and have her sinful way with him. The moment of opportunity vanished when Jake turned as if he made a sudden decision. "Come." His hand motioned for her to come forward. "Stand in front of the mirror."

She stood firm not liking where this was going. Hannah didn't take orders.

He removed his jacket, his penetrating stare never leaving hers "I said, stand in front of the mirror."

She finally obeyed but only because she was curious to see what he was going to do.

He unbuttoned his shirt with a confidence that unnerved her—like he had a plan of action that nothing would stop him from seeing it through. His body sculpted like the Gods of the past belonged in a museum to be admired by all and blushed over by teenage girls. Unlike many athletes his body remained untouched by a tattoo pen. Tossing the shirt to the bed he came to stand behind her.

His lips grazed her shoulder as he played with the strap of her dress. The expression on his face was one of conflict. Would he rip off the dress or simply take it off? Anticipation built inside of her until SHE wanted to tear it off. But Jake did neither, pulling her hair loose.

This was going way too slow. Every part of her ached with desire—with need.

He brought a handful of her hair to his nose and breathed deep. "My Hannah Rose."

How did he know her middle name? She turned to look at him.

"Eyes on the mirror."

Again he toyed with the strap before sliding it down her arm, kissing her shoulder again. "You look like a delicious stick of cotton candy. I'm going to make you melt in my mouth."

Way. Too. Slow. She'd prefer if he gobbled her up instead.

Pulling the other strap down, he kissed that shoulder adding a lick. "Taste like it too."

Kisses trailed down her spine. The tug at the zipper left her bottom exposed to more kisses. Her knees buckled but he held onto her hips.

Coming back up he pulled the dress down over her breasts and the gown pooled at her feet. His fingers swept down the curve of her spine to her bottom and he rubbed the swell of her cheeks before taking off her thong.

"Now lean against me."

As if she could do anything else as his hand slid down her torso to the apex of her thighs. Photo shoot ready her pussy was shaven and already glistening with wetness.

"Have you ever looked at yourself?"

Hannah knew what he meant—down there. "Not lately."

"It's pink and plump – like a piece of cotton candy." Spreading the folds of her sex, Jake used his middle finger in a circular motion on her nub. "See?"

Erotic feelings erupted within her as she watched Jake's magic fingers tease her into a frenzy; she looked up for a moment to his hungry gazed locked on her pussy. His finger increased the pressure but used the same agonizing slowness, then fast, and then when she came to the brink he slowed again. His solid body supported her weight and her bottom ground against his erection urging for more than his fingers. His other hand played with her breast, teasing the nipple between his fingers.

"Jake. Jake." Hannah tugged on her lip so she wouldn't whimper.

His deep timber voice wrapped around her like a cloak of passion pushing her higher and higher until she feared there'd be no release. "That's it Hannah, say my name, over and over again until it becomes a prayer. Until I'm your God and I'll make you my Goddess."

Who talks like that? Any other man and she would've laughed in his face. But she wasn't laughing. She was coming. Delicious power jolted through her insides. "That's it, baby." He pulled her closer. "Look in the mirror and see what I see when I make you come."

She did and the feral look in his eyes undid her. The power drained from her body as she sobbed his name. Her knees gave out but Jake was right there scooping her up and gently laid her on the bed.

Why couldn't he be just another dumb jock looking for a quick lay? But then she wouldn't have experienced this. Whatever this was. Bliss? Heaven? There was no name.

Hannah enjoyed sex, but with Jake, enjoy didn't cover it. Didn't even scratch the surface of what she was feeling. And he hadn't even used his mouth. Yet.

Jake wet his lips with his tongue like he was getting ready to indulge in a delicacy. But it was Hannah who wanted the treat. Normally, she didn't take a man into her mouth. Such activities were hell on the skin, causing wrinkles and breakouts.

But she wanted to taste Jake. Wanted him to be the one to moan her name. Wanted him to feel the way he made her feel. To make him feel like a king and enslave him all at the same time. When Jake moved to lie down, she sat back up and stood on wobbly legs. He held her steady. Regaining her balance she maneuvered him back to the mirror with one hand while the other worked at his belt. Tugging it through the loops of his pants she purred, "Your turn."

The belt came free and she snapped it as if she were Catwoman.

"Oh God."

Hannah licked her lips as she pulled down his zipper while rubbing the tips of her breast against his chest. "God's got nothing to do with it."

Chapter 6

J ake swallowed hard as Hannah made short work of his pants, shoes, and socks. His erection jutted out, ready for anything that she had in mind. With Hannah still in her heels she was taller than he was.

She surveyed him like she was a Dom and he her Sub. "Stand sideways," she ordered.

He arched an eyebrow but did as he was told. For now.

She took a frilly pink pillow from the bed and tossed it at his feet. "You're going to watch as I take you in my mouth."

That mouth. He would last all of ten seconds. In fact if she didn't stop talking about it he'd be done. Stepping closer her hands roamed over his shoulders, down his abs, lingering a moment before wrapping her fingers around his cock. "Do you think I can take all of you in?"

"Hannah," he breathed.

Catching the breath in a kiss she took his tongue into her mouth and sucked. A bead of come sprung to the tip of his cock and with her finger she spread it around the head moaning with deep satisfaction. "Now look who's wet for who." An evil feline smile lit up her face. "Do you have any idea how hungry I am?"

Instead of being intimidated by the question he grew harder in her hand. "That's good, I have a lot to feast on."

"That you do," she said sliding to her knees.

With nothing to hold on to Jake planted his body in a stance that the largest linebacker in the NFL couldn't take down. But then Hannah's lips encircled his cock; he swayed like an Oak sapling in a hurricane.

Sweet, slow, and deep, with no rush, Hannah seemed to savor each stroke almost as much as he did. Almost. He wasn't going to last, wasn't going to make it to the fast and furious pumping of her mouth. If she even flicked her tongue he'd spill every drop.

Jake averted his gaze to the ceiling and recited the new playbook inside his head. Hannah must have felt the brief disconnect and stopped.

"Look in the mirror, Jake."

His cock jumped, demanding to be back in the warm, wet heaven of Hannah's mouth. Looking back to the mirror he caught Hannah's misty gaze. Her blue eyes, which always reminded him of the sky, now matched the flowing waters of the Caribbean. She smiled a pure feminine smile like a woman who knew all the mysteries of the world. As far as his cock was concerned she did.

Her swollen lips surrounded him again. The sight of her kneeling naked, her full breasts jiggling slightly as she moved back and forth tore him in two—one half the Emperor of the Universe who wanted Hannah to pleasure him until he exploded in her mouth, the other half beast who wanted to throw her on the bed on all fours and take her from behind—which side would win?

Hannah picked up the pace and what was once one torturous long stroke after another became short and rapid.

The pressure built and it felt like every drop of blood in his body had rushed to join the party. His legs quivered like he finished sprinting down a hundred football fields. Just when he thought he'd fall to the floor in defeat she slowed and swallowed him whole, settling his cock in the back of her throat. Enough. He needed to be inside her right now. To make her feel alive with want until it became a need that only he could fill. Grabbing at her hair he pulled her away.

"I'm not done yet." Hannah pouted.

"Don't move." Jake opened the nightstand drawer where Hannah kept an arsenal of condoms. He hoped in the past seven months she hadn't had a reason to re-stock it. The thought caused possessive feelings to swell up in his chest. He wanted to claim her. Put his mark on her. Wanted her in the most primitive position found in the animal kingdom.

Kneeling behind Hannah, he shifted them both so they faced the mirror.

"Oh!" The surprise on Hannah's face when he entered her was priceless. He pulled her up to rest her body against his chest so he could see and play with her breasts while he moved in and out of her. It would be an awkward position for a couple if the man wasn't well hung. But his size allowed for deep penetration.

Hannah drew in deep breaths like she was getting ready to dive under the sea and not come up. She was close. So was he.

"I'll never forget this moment, Hannah." *Never.* With that he reached down and played with her clit as he continued to pump in and out of her, unleashing the beast inside him and roaring his climax. From far away he heard Hannah scream his name. They collapsed together on the floor, falling into a tangled embrace, their bodies still shuddering. He kissed her hair, breathing in the scent of candy. Little purrs escaped her lips. He reached down and tapped her nub. Another orgasm hit her—short and hard. He shifted to study her wild and lovely form. Her honeyed hair splayed against the floor. Perfect size C breasts, a slender tummy that swelled to curvy hips made for a man to thrust against. The beauty to his beast. His mate.

He wanted her again. Now.

Forever.

Whoa! Where the hell did that come from?

A great blowjob made men stupid. History was littered with men who gave up their freedom, hell, who fought wars all because they couldn't separate their cock from their heart. That's all this was. Tomorrow he'd wake up and be back to Jake Miller, lady-killer.

He shouldn't take any chances and leave now. Tell her he had to get up early for—whatever. Damn, he couldn't even think straight. Then Hannah curled up and snuggled against him and his arms automatically wound around her. She sighed with contentment, which filled Jake with an unexpected sense of fulfillment.

Jake lay sprawled on the empty bed. The smell of coffee wafted in but nothing short of Armageddon could get him up. Noises from the kitchen built up his hopes for breakfast in bed.

In the morning light he studied the bedroom. Hannah definitely had a thing for pink. And lace. And sparkling things. But the bed was big and so damn comfortable.

Fluffy pillows tossed from the bed last night laid strewn about the room and the soft comforter wrapped around his legs slid along his skin reminding him of Hannah's touch. The room smelled of her. And of sex. Yeah, it would take Armageddon to get him out of bed. At 6'3" he must look ridiculous laid out on her bed. Or whipped.

Holy shit!

Jake leaned up on his arms and locked about the room.

This is a lair!

A lair belonging to a sexy siren worthy of any mythological story and like Odysseus, Jake would need to be tied to a mast to keep him away from the siren's song. He half expected a spider web to be spun around him at any moment.

Jake sprung out of bed just to be sure.

He used the bathroom, noting the various potions to lure a man into bed. Perfume, skin cream, and make-up. Pulling on his briefs, then his pants, he escaped to the kitchen where another smell—an unpleasant one invaded his senses.

A grumpy Hannah looked up from a plate of steamed asparagus.

"What the hell?"

"Breakfast of Supermodels. Yum. Yum." The grimace on her face as she took a bite said it all "I made you coffee. I'd make you some eggs but I'm afraid I might eat them." Waving a floppy spear of asparagus in the air she said, "This is all I can eat today. Gets rid of swelly belly."

"You belly is sexy."

"The camera doesn't think so."

"You don't take any pills?" He turned to pour a cup of coffee so she wouldn't see the concern that he knew was etched on his face.

"No! I just get, get..."

"Bitchy," he risked. Turning back he caught the narrowing of Hannah's eyes.

"I was going to say cranky."

Jake threw back his head and laughed.

Hannah took another bite and made a yucky face.

He should keep his mouth shut. They were getting along, laughing together, having mind blowing sex and besides it was none of his business how she ran her life. But he worried about her so he was making it his business. He took the seat across from her. "That's not healthy."

"Asparagus is very healthy."

"You know what I mean. The dieting. You're starving yourself."

"Oh, and you keep those 8 pack abs by drinking beer and eating donuts?"

"Food is fuel for the body. When you look at it like that it's easy to make the right choices."

"I've been making my own choices all by myself for a long time. Besides, I believe in fitness not famine."

Hannah's bitchy tone didn't fool Jake because the pained look in her eyes did not escape his notice. "For how long?"

"Since I was sixteen."

"What?" Jake nearly shouted. The thought of her so young and alone triggered every protective instinct within him. He calmed and in a gentler tone asked, "Where were your parents?"

"Look, you can just Google it. I'm sure all the sordid details are still there."

"I'd rather hear it from you."

The doorbell rang. "That must be my yoga instructor. Can you answer the door so I can get ready?"

"Sure, but this talk isn't over."

Opening the door halfway to a good-looking guy holding a mat, Jake leaned his arm against the doorframe like he owned the place. Glad he was still shirtless, he made sure to flex a muscle to intimidate the instructor. "Can I help you?"

"I'm here for Hannah's lesson."

Jake opened the door the rest of the way to let him in. He hated how the guy knew his way around Hannah's living room. His fists tightened wondering if he knew the bedroom as well.

Hannah came bounding out wearing yoga pants and a t-shirt. "Thanks Jake."

"I'm gonna hit the shower." *A long shower.* He'd learned long ago to take himself out of situations that would trigger his temper. But there was no way he was leaving this apartment.

All dressed, Jake left the bedroom to see the 'instructors' hands on Hannah's hips, fingertips away from her curvy ass as she bent over into a carnal position that only *HE* should be putting her in. The muscle in his jaw twitched. Needing every anger management skill he learned he calmed himself with a deep breath.

Still, he probably would have said something, hell he probably would've punched something, but Hannah jumped up from the pose and ran over and kissed him with the same wild abandon she showed last night on the red carpet. He gladly returned it, claiming her in front of Mr. Tight Pants. "See you tonight?"

"I need my beauty sleep for the shoot tomorrow and I won't get much sleep if you're here." Hannah giggled.

The yoga instructor cleared his throat.

"I'll be right back." Hannah walked Jake to the door.

"Tomorrow night then. Say 7:00?"

"Yes, but dinner first. I'm going to eat the world tomorrow."

Jake kissed her goodbye but before he closed the door he asked, "Would it be Medieval of me to ask that you switch to a female yoga instructor?" He hated himself for showing any sign of weakness. It would be wiser to stay away from the woman who made his blood burn, but he was too captivated by her to do anything about it. The siren had him well and truly snared.

"Because you actually asked, no it wouldn't be." Hannah closed the door leaving him wondering if she would or not.

Chapter 7

Hannah closed the door with a smile and almost skipped into the living room where the dour face of Raphael stopped her dead. "What?"

"He told you to get rid of me, didn't he?"

"Of course, he's not an idiot. And for your information he asked."

"He's no good for you. Once the season starts he'll go back to his groupies when you're not around."

Hannah had the same thought but that didn't mean she would let Raphael bad mouth Jake. "And you're any better? Don't think I don't know how you hit it and quit it." The instructor looked away as she continued. "And that you've been biding your time until you made your move or I made mine."

Raphael rolled up his mat. "Yet you kept me around."

One of her model friends recommended Raphael as a cure all to getting over an ex, but despite his pretty boy looks, long locks that a rock star would be jealous of, and the lithe body of a yogi, his touch did nothing to her insides. Not even a spark. Nothing. "Only because it amused me." And because she hoped her feelings would change.

"You're heartless."

Hannah disagreed. She had a heart, only it belonged to Jake. *What?*

No, no, no she wasn't it love. No way. Impossible. It was just the afterglow of nuclear hot sex and now she was experiencing a meltdown. "Yes, so you see there's no need to worry about whether Jake is good for me or not."

"All men are weak when it comes to the opposite sex," said Raphael. He strode to the door but turned back before shutting it, "Even me. So when he breaks your heart you have my number."

Hannah would feel a smidgen of guilt for how she treated Raphael if she didn't know what a player he was. His comments about Jake were merely sour grapes. She resumed her yoga workout since she had an hour to kill until the Pilates instructor showed up. After that an hour on the treadmill since running the streets of NYC invited the paparazzi to harass her. It took an army of personal trainers, assistants, and skin care specialists to keep Hannah Hahn supermodel ready. It was a full-time job especially as she'd gotten older, but she didn't mind. How could she? Money. Travel. Fame. Men. Until seven months ago that is. Now she only wanted one.

Coming out the Salamba Sirsasana pose she eased to the floor and stared at the ceiling. Even yoga couldn't quiet her mind. Raphael was right. Expecting a normal male to stay monogamous was an act of faith, but football players?—an act of lunacy. As long as she kept that in that back of her head, her heart would remain safe. She'd enjoy the sex and when it was over, it was over. Who knows maybe she'd be the one to get bored first. That was her M.O. But those men didn't compare to Jake. Not even close.

The phone rang. Not planning to answer the phone since she'd rather brood, her mood lifted immediately when the caller id flashed. Samantha? She pushed the speaker and teased, "Honeymoon over already?"

"Ha, ha. Ryan is convalescing," bragged Samantha.

"You go girl." Hannah flounced onto the comfy white couch.

"Never mind me. What's going on with you?"

"Nothing," said Hannah. Samantha and Ryan had waited along time to be together and she wouldn't worry her with any drama—at least not on her honeymoon.

"I saw the twitter photo."

"You follow me?"

"Don't evade. Spill!"

So Hannah did. "We'll see how long it lasts this time."

"Oh Hannah, don't lead him on."

Taken aback she asked, "Lead him on?"

"If you saw what a big mope he was without you, you'd understand. He was pathetic."

Hannah heard a clearing of a throat clear across the phone line from Ireland. Ryan.

"Uh-oh, you're giving away top secret guy information."

"It's no secret that Jake is half in love with you."

"Yeah, the half with his penis."

Samantha laughed, but said, "If the penis loves you then the heart will soon follow. Then sometime after that, his brain will realize it. It's a complicated process."

Hannah may not have the faith, but a small bit of hope welled up inside her.

Samantha pressed the end key and turned to face her husband. Lounging against the numerous pillows in the enormous canopy bed and bedding colored in a rich maroon, Ryan looked like the Lord of Castle Durrow.

"Convalescing, am I?"

'You mean you're ready for more?" Samantha climbed up onto the bed.

"Hell, yeah. Gotta get it in now. When we get back it's straight to training camp for me."

At some point they were going to have to actually leave the room and explore the castle and the grounds. *At some point.*

Hannah waited impatiently for the lights to be reset. She needed to eat and hydrate, but more than that she needed Jake. She missed his large body taking up the whole bed while he slept. She missed the deep, silken voice that made her want to lose her clothes. Pronto. And that sexy smile that promised wicked, wicked things.

Her phone vibrated in the pocket of the robe that covered her up while she waited for the shoot to resume. With lightning speed she answered it. "Jake?"

"What are you wearing?"

Tingles of excitement lit up her body. "That's top secret."

"Tell me now, kill me later."

Hannah laughed. "Just my uniform, a bra and panties."

"Nothing on you is just anything."

"Well..." She teased. "I'm wearing push-up bra in a deep blue, almost purple color with a black lace design sewn over it."

"And the panties?"

Oh boy, it was a good thing she got to keep them. Hannah rubbed her legs together to ease the growing ache. "Cut low with a black lace bow."

"A bow I can pull open like a present?"

"Jake," she breathed into the phone.

"Well?"

"Maybe."

"Such a tease."

"Look who's talking?"

"Do I get a sneak preview when you come home?"

Home? He made it sound like he belonged there. "You'll have to wait and see." She heard her named called. "I'm needed back on set."

"When you're posing Hannah, think of me. Think of me sliding down the bra strap, leaving little kisses behind and—"

"Oh, that is so not fair."

"See ya tonight, baby doll."

Hannah slipped off the robe and sashayed over to her mark like she was on the runaway. She was going to rock the rest of this shoot. Sending smoldering looks to the camera her inner vixen clawed out of hiding.

"Wow, I'm surprised the lens didn't catch fire. Must be that football player you're dating," teased Michael.

Michael was one of her favorite photographers. He loved the female form and not in a sexual way. For him, she knew, it was all about the art.

"Must be."

He'd been the first to shoot her after a harrowing experience with a photographer who preyed upon young and naïve models, with promises to make them famous. All the more harrowing because her mother demanded Hannah do as the man said and strip off her clothes. "It's Paris, Hannah, it's okay here." It didn't feel okay. She'd been fifteen.

Michael sensed her fear and the reason behind it. He advised her and gave her tools to handle herself in the future. Then he threatened her mother with Child Protective Services.

"He's on my fantasy football team. I heard he's being traded."

"Fantasy football?" Hannah had no idea what this implied but Jake didn't mention anything about a trade. She tried to keep the panic out of her voice. "Jake still has a year on his contract."

"He's looking for more cash. He's threatening to holdout and the Cougars are threatening to trade him."

A spear of hurt struck her heart. All this was happening in his life and he didn't tell her never mind discuss it with her. The hurt turned to anger. It was bad enough that once the season started they'd be apart for long stretches with his away games and her modeling assignments, but another city? It would never work. "We don't exactly talk business."

"Who could blame him?"

Hannah could. Grabbing her phone she set up a text to Jake and hit the send key. 'Have headache...tonight is off'. To which he promptly replied, "?". Hannah ignored it, like he ignored her. How dare he start a relationship with her when he knew he might be traded? Was this part of his game plan? A trade would provide him with an easy exit. Perhaps, even payback for dumping him.

In the dressing room she changed into her next outfit. She wished she could call Samantha to talk about trades and holdouts. And if she didn't know as the former beat reporter for the Cougars then Ryan should know what was going on in his teammates mind.

An inner voice urged her to let Jake explain but she feigned inner deafness. Looking in the mirror she noted the frown lines creasing into her forehead. Relationships were rough on the skin.

On the heart they were hell.

Chapter 8

Upon hearing the slam to the front door of Hannah's apartment, Jake slid the pasta into the boiling water and then stirred the meatballs simmering in a pot of his Mom's famous sauce. Listening for the voices of Nate and Hannah he stood by the archway opening of the kitchen that led to the living room hoping for a heads up on why Hannah was pissed at him. Jake racked his brain for the past few hours but came up with nothing. He'd been the perfect boyfriend.

"What's that glorious smell?" Hannah's honeyed voice filter down the hall.

"Jake is cooking dinner," said Nate.

"Like right now?"

"Yes, I called him."

"I texted you instructions and they did not include interfering in my love life."

Jake winced at the terseness in her voice.

"I'm your assistant thereby I'm assisting you in not ruining your life!"

Should he go out there? Nate shouldn't be taking the heat for this. He couldn't make cut what Hannah said next but what Nate said in response was crystal clear.

"I will not stand for another seven months of you being a bitch."

Silence. Jake arched an eyebrow. Was someone dead?

Jake heard Hannah burst out into tears. "I'm sorry, Nate."

"Oh, sweetie, don't cry."

"Why do you put up with me?" More sobbing.

Jake wondered if she was PMS'ing. That would explain everything.

"Cause I'm your gay guardian angel in disguise. Now, go talk to him. No, wait. Go, LISTEN."

Jake returned to the stove, turned off the heat under the sauce, and stirred the pasta one more time.

She turned the corner and walked right over to him with her arms folded in a defensive gesture. "Jake we have to—"

He cut her off with a spoonful of sauce.

"Mmmm, that is delicious!" Her arms relaxed to her sides. "We have to talk," she said softly.

He smiled at the effect of his mother's creation. Perhaps he should send a jar over to the United Nations. "After we eat, when you're not feeling so…cranky."

Hannah smirked before turning to the table. "Oh!"

Jake went all out. Tablecloth, cloth napkins, candles, china and silverware and of course flowers. For a moment he worried about her getting the wrong idea. The scene was set for a proposal.

"Did Nate help you?"

"He just got me in the door." Jake pulled out a chair.

Hannah smiled sweetly but sat down in the other seat. Holding his frustration in check he readied the rest of the meal and poured the wine. He took the seat that she didn't and they ate in silence—except for the little moans of pleasure escaping her mouth. His crotch tightened and he hoped 'the talk' didn't take too long. Figuring she'd take a couple of bites and feign a full stomach, he was impressed with the amount she consumed.

Her plate was nearly empty when she said, "Why didn't you tell me about the trade?"

Jake leaned back in his seat and chuckled. "That's what this is about?" However, Hannah didn't seem amused.

"You make it sound like it's not important. Like I'm not important enough to discuss your life with."

"Its a game, Hannah. The team will flinch. I'm not going anywhere." He leaned forward and reached for her hand. "Anywhere."

"You don't know that for sure." She snatched her hand away. "I shouldn't have to find out from someone else. You need to communicate."

That word was a curse on men. "We've been busy."

"Gee, you had time to lecture me on my diet."

From the opening of the kitchen Nate said, "Just tell her you were wrong."

"Nate!"

"I'm going. I'm going."

Jake laughed. "He's a good friend."

After taking a sip of wine she said, "I don't know whether to hug him or fire him."

"I think we all know the answer to that."

"Hmm, that doesn't mean I want to hug you at this moment—or anything else." She took another bite of pasta.

Jake wasn't about to heed Nate's advice and apologize. It would set a bad precedent and besides it wasn't like he cheated or forgot her birthday. "Look, going forward I'll update you on the contract talks."

Hannah looked away and didn't seem satisfied with his compromise, so he decided to push back a little. "And it's not like you came clean when I asked what happened between you and your parents."

"That is ancient history."

"Not when it's sitting here at the table like a third wheel." And there it was—the reason he needed to know. The reason he pushed. He couldn't slay her dragons if he couldn't see them.

Annoyed how he expertly turned this around on her, she also acknowledged that communication was a two way street. For her, it was a road less traveled so Hannah weighed each word carefully so she wouldn't reveal too much. "I was eleven when my father left. My mother was thirty-five. He found a younger version of her and took off to Vegas." She reached for the wine and poured. The easiest part of her story was over with and hopefully he wouldn't dig any deeper.

"So you have daddy issues?"

The glass of wine halted midway to her lips. "I have parental issues." Bringing the glass the rest of the way she down the contents like a sailor instead of a supermodel.

"What's the deal with your Mom?"

Shame and embarrassment caused Hannah to examine the place mat, to look anywhere but at Jake. "When I was sixteen my mother said derogatory—no hateful remarks regarding an African-American who received a national campaign over me." If she looked up would she see judgment in his eyes? The color of his skin, which Hannah found so intoxicating, would cause her mother to shudder in revulsion.

"The modeling agency threw my mother out of the building. On the way home she turned her rant on me, calling me fat and put me on a diet. At least that's what she calls starvation. It was a week later after passing out in school that Social Services stepped in."

She risked a glance but then his gaze held hers captive.

Were those tears forming in his eyes or merely a reflection of her gaze? She shot up out of her seat and with shaky hands placed the plate in the sink, then held onto the counter for dear life as she rushed on with the rest. "Anyway, I was allowed to emancipate myself with the help of Samantha's parents and the agency hired a chaperone for overseas assignments until I was eighteen."

Hannah would never reveal the rest of her pathetic history.

She turned to clean off the rest of the table but Jake was right there wrapping her up in a tight embrace. He smoothed her hair as he brushed a kiss on her forehead. The tears that threatened spilled onto her cheeks. Scooping her up into his arms he carried her into the bedroom as if she weighed nothing more than a child. Putting her down, he tilted her chin. Soft light reflected in his eyes making them appear layered in amber.

"You are amazing, Hannah. Even with shit for parents you became a successful and giving woman."

"But I'm still a mess."

"Everyone is."

"Even you?"

Ah, crap. I walked right into that one.

Despite the oh-so-innocent eyes looking at him she did exactly what he did a few minutes ago, redirected the conversation. Perhaps it was best to get the past out into the open and deal with it so they could get on to more pleasurable activities. He motioned for her to sit down. "I have a juvie record."

"What did you do?"

"I beat up my older brother's tormentor."

"Your older brother?"

"I was thirteen—a large thirteen. My brother was fifteen. And gay." Confused over Vinnie's sexual orientation and angry with his father for leaving the family because of it, Jake released it all in a fury of fists on the boy who taunted his brother.

"That's so sweet. And stupid."

He sat down next to her. "Like I said, I was thirteen." He learned quickly that he couldn't fight his brother's battles. Over time the confusion became clarity and he channeled the anger at his father onto the football field.

"So any parental issues?"

He wouldn't tell her how his father blamed his mother nor about the night he left leaving Jake with a black eye to toughen him up so as his father put it 'you don't end up a fag like your brother.' Some things you just don't talk about. "None."

"Commitment issues?"

"Not fair, we've both got that one."

"Okay, then why me? Why now?"

"Because it hurts more to stay away." *Shut up, Jake. Shut up now. Shut up before you tell her you love her. Bring it back to sex.* The day had been hell and all he wanted to do was lose himself inside her and find Heaven again.

Hannah climbed onto his lap, straddling him and wrapping her legs around him. His hands naturally drifted to her ass.

"I was miserable too, you know."

Their gazes locked. One week of bliss, then seven months of hell, of being a blind man granted sight then it cruelly taken away. Could he survive it again? Better to have love and lost than to never have loved at all. *Bullshit!*

Determined not to lose, he stood with her in his arms and then kneeled on the bed sliding her off to lie on her back before him. Needing her naked and exposed he yanked the two sides of her button down shirt apart. The sight before him made him pause in wonder. "Ah, you're wearing it."

"It gave me a twisted satisfaction to think you wouldn't see it."

"You're evil."

A saucy smile appeared on her face. "Yes, but in a good way."

Laughing he helped her shimmy out of her jeans. And there they were, the panties that he'd been thinking about all day. All it would take is a slight tug on the bow for all to be revealed. "I feel like a kid on Christmas morning."

"Were you a good boy?"

"Apparently I was." He twirled the ribbon around his finger then pulled on the ribbon and the lacy fabric parted to the V of her clit. "I think Victoria Secret has a bestseller here."

"I'll tell marketing."

"You won't be able to form a coherent sentence when I'm done with you."

"You're all talk. No tongue."

He trailed kisses along the curves of her body. Upon reaching the edges of her panties his tongue slipped in. Her hips arched begging for more. Inspired by the ribbon he rubbed the fabric back and forth between the folds of her sex as his tongue continued to flick.

"Jake, Jake, Jake," she panted.

Blood raged through his body as she called his name over and over again. Even eighty thousand fans chanting his name never made him feel so amped.

The moment he added pressure her legs clamped around his head. The shuddering of Hannah's body sent waves of vibrations through his. The sweet elixir of her essence became apart of him, a drink of the Gods.

In record time he lost his pants and rolled on a condom. Stretching his body on top of hers he entered her soft wetness.

Hannah's closed eyes fluttered open. "Jake, I…that was amazing."

Her unshed tears broke him. Was she about to tell him she loved him? Suddenly he knew if she chose to stomp all over his heart he'd let her.

Eyes locked together he moved with slow but deep strokes and for once she didn't beg for more. There would be no frantic end this time. If they were both too afraid to say it with words then their bodies spoke of the love between them until the passion became too much and they trembled into each other's arms.

Minutes later Jake was barely conscious when Hannah who seemed filled with enough energy to go ten rounds asked, "Jake, what's fantasy football?"

Chapter 9

Hannah relaxed into Janu Sirsasana, a head-to-knee forward yoga pose, while Samantha struggled into the position. With Jake at training camp and with no modeling assignments until next week she had hours upon hours to fill. So did her best friend who whined over the phone about missing Ryan. Hannah invited her to the apartment to share a yoga session with her new instructor, Theresa. Then at lunch Samantha would teach Hannah about football. If she wanted to survive as a celebrity girlfriend to a NFL football player she needed to know her x's and o's. Being perceived as Jake's dumb supermodel arm candy is not an image she wished to encourage. Even though Jake explained it in detail, she still didn't comprehend the attraction of fantasy football. But Jake didn't complain when she showed him her version of the game.

In the background the TV was on mute with the channel set on a local sports station. Hannah was hoping to catch a glimpse of Jake. Saying goodbye to him was like saying goodbye to a part of herself and she wouldn't be whole again until he came home. Yes, home. They were living together though neither of them said it out loud.

Was he missing her? Was he even thinking about her?

They moved into the next position and she held in a laugh as Theresa tried to bend Samantha into the Camel Pose.

"That's it. I can't do this!" Samantha untangled herself. "I'm not Gumby, you know."

"Oh, come on. Ryan will love the new flexibility," Hannah teased.

"That's true," said Theresa in a woman of the world wisdom tone.

"I have other skills," replied Samantha in an equally sage voice.

Hannah hooted. "I bet you do!"

"I'm grabbing something to eat. You do have food, don't you?"

"Yes, I even have ice cream." Freaking men. Last night she wallowed into a pint of Rocky Road.

"Wow, it must be love. No man has driven you to ice cream," said Samantha as she left the room.

"I'm not in love, merely horny."

Hannah heard Samantha snort from the kitchen. Theresa started to work with her but out of the corner of her eye Jake appeared on the screen. "Wait!" The instructor stepped back as Hannah reached for the remote to turn the volume on.

"You two are impossible to work with!"

Hannah barely noticed Theresa packing up to leave. The reporter was interviewing Jake outside a campus building about his fat new contract and in the background several college girls in skimpy summer clothes lingered. "Samantha, do you still have your press credentials?" she shouted.

"Yes. Why?" she called back from the kitchen.

"I think we should crash training camp."

Samantha came into the living room licking peanut butter off a spoon. "Not even wives are allowed-." She nearly walked into Hannah who was pointing to the TV. "They might as well be wearing bikinis!"

"Road trip?"

"You better get used to it now. Once the season starts it will get worse," advised Samantha.

"I know, but I miss him. If I devour another pint of ice cream I'm going to explode." The reporter turned to speak to Ryan and Hannah pointed to the TV. "Come on, don't you miss him?"

Samantha nodded but said, "We might get them into trouble with the coaches."

"Yeah, but we're worth it."

An hour later they were heading out of the city. A road trip in Ryan's 350I was a lot different than the time they took to the highway in Samantha's beat up pickup truck the summer after their high school graduation. The car, the clothes, hairstyles may be different but they were still the same girls hoping for adventure.

"Have you told him?"

"What?"

"That you love him."

"Hell, no. Not going to either." Hannah cranked up the radio to tune out any further inquires from the former reporter, turned author, who was known for getting people to talk. Some people called her the Obi-Wan of journalists. Hannah called her nosy.

Three hours later they pulled into the parking lot of the college campus where the Cougars held their two-week training camp every summer. Jake said it helped the players focus solely on football without outside distractions, and bonded them together as a team, as a family. Hannah tried to understand but she was never a part of something like that. Modeling was more of a solitary endeavor, competing with other models for the gig. Yes there were photographers and makeup artists but truthfully the product she was selling was more important than she was.

And family? What little she knew of them came from the Jamesons.

Samantha turned off the engine. "Okay, now what?"

"I was thinking you could sneak me into one of the training rooms while they are out on the field then I'll text him my location."

"Wow, you have this all figured out, except no phones on the field."

"Can you get onto the field and talk to him?"

Samantha reached over to the glove box. "What good are my press credentials if I can't use them to help you score?"

"Hey, you got to see a locker room full of naked men."

"For my job. And they weren't all naked." Samantha opened the car door and got out.

Hannah followed suit and said, "Still."

"Believe me the fantasy is better than the reality."

"OMG! I just thought of something. You saw Jake's penis!"

"Like I said they weren't all naked, so some were." said Samantha with a wink.

Which didn't answer Hannah's question, but the facial expression on her friend's face did.

★   ★   ★

Samantha ignored Ryan's questioning stare by watching Jake sprint to the building where Hannah waited for him. She hoped no one from the team's staff wandered into the building and catches the two in a compromising position.

"What's going on?" asked Ryan.

She turned to her new husband, a little miffed that he didn't seem happy to see her. "We were watching the morning news. Hannah freaked out when a bunch of scantly dressed college girls were waiting in the background like vultures."

"Just Hannah?"

"Yep. I'm just along for the ride."

"Liar."

"Okay, maybe I was a little jealous."

"Terell, no wives!" The coach screamed from across the field.

Samantha winced. She used to be a foreign correspondent, then the Cougars beat reporter and now she was relegated to a mere football wife.

"She's here on business." Ryan shouted back.

"Then she should know better, no reporters on the field during practice."

"You better go before I get fined or worse."

Samantha resisted kissing Ryan goodbye in front of his teammates and coaches but did smack him on the ass before turning to leave the field.

"You'll pay for that one Mrs. Terell "

"Counting on it."

Ryan caught up with her and pulled right into a kiss. The honeymoon was definitely not over. A perfect blend of sweetness and passion his kiss made it clear he missed her. He pulled away, his eyes still filled with the same intensity as the first time he kissed her.

"You know you have nothing to worry about."

"I know." Samantha left the field to go up into the stands to wait for Hannah hoping that she and Jake were headed for their own happy ever after.

Chapter 10

J ake knew he was going to catch shit about going MIA, but when Samantha said Hannah needed to see him he wasn't about to ignore the invitation. What possessed her to drive all the way up here? He made it clear this wasn't a vacation. Instead of training camp it should be called boot camp. The practice from hell left him sweaty and dirty. Nothing he could do about it, Hannah would have to take him as he was. The click, clack of his cleats sounded against the linoleum floor. Not exactly what he'd call a clandestine meeting. He reached the door and peered through the glass side panel to see Hannah pacing back and forth in the team meeting room. His eyes were naturally drawn to the flounce of her yellow skirt each time she turned. Those sleek legs enticed him as much as what laid beneath the skirt. He took a deep breath before opening the door to prepare for the onslaught of sexual urges he was already having trouble controlling.

It'd been a long week without those lips on his, without burying himself deep inside her. She turned as he entered, those big blue eyes brightened to a hue that an artist would be hard pressed to capture and the smile so huge and genuine it nearly knocked him to his knees.

"Oh Jake!" Hannah rushed him and jumped into his arms.

He hugged her close and said into her neck. "What are you doing here?"

"You don't miss me?"

Was she crazy? "Every damn moment."

"Well, me, too." She smashed his lips with a kiss.

He fumbled to shut the door as she grabbed at the strings of his pants. "Whoa, is this a booty call?" He couldn't keep the amazement out of his voice.

"No, I had Samantha drive me 3 hours to say hello." Hannah pulled him over to the desk in the corner as she continued to work on the strings.

Jake backed her up against the desk kissing her like he hadn't seen her in forever instead of a few days. The scent of flowers surrounded him clashing with his stink. "I'm sweaty."

"It's kind of hot." She pulled out his cock and her hand ran down its full length. "Make me sweat too."

His cock twitched in her hand. From there it got hot and heavy. Clothes pulled aside for access while allowing for a quick retreat if they were caught. "Ah, Hannah, I don't I have much time for foreplay."

"I'm beyond foreplay."

"Condom?"

"Oh, I didn't think about that. Do you have one?"

"It's training camp, beautiful, not a college dorm party."

For a moment only the sound of their heavy breaths filled the space. "Well, we should be okay."

He didn't question it. With Hannah's aversion to gaining weight and her career at a peak he knew the last thing she wanted was a pregnancy. Down the line that might be an issue, but right now? It didn't matter. All that matter was being inside her. Day after day of drills left him exhausted. But night after night he thought of her until he fell asleep and then she came to him in his dreams. And now she was here.

Hannah bent over the desk but he maneuvered her into a sitting position of the desk. "I want to see you." For her it might be a booty call, but for him it meant she needed him as much as he needed her. Pulling aside her panties he pushed inside her. Usually he had more finesse but Hannah wasn't here for tenderness so he gave her what she wanted and pounded into her.

"Yes, Jake, yes."

Her pleas turned him on. Everything about her did. He could do this for hours, just pleasing her, but time was of the essence. Anyone could walk down the hall and hear them. Hell, as Hannah's moans grew louder he wouldn't be surprised to learn the whole team down at the field heard them. "Come for me Hannah. Now."

She shuddered around him causing his own climax. As he came to his senses he realized how rough he'd been with her. Jake gently stoked her cheek. "You, okay? I didn't hurt you?"

"Did it sound like you hurt me?"

"I don't know. It could go either way."

Hannah blushed. "Dirty sex with you doesn't feel dirty. It makes me feel, I don't know, cleansed?" She pulled away and started re-adjusting her clothes.

Jake wondered if sex was all that kept them together. He shook his head to clear his mind. He was thinking like a woman. A most disturbing thought. He laced up his pants. "I'm going to be a sack of shit the rest of practice."

"Not even Superman has your stamina." Hannah smoothed her hair back.

He liked it better messed up, especially if he was the cause of it. "I can't figure out whether you're my Lois Lane or my Kryptonite."

"Neither. I'm Wonder Woman, your equal."

"I definitely met my match in you." Liking the comparison he smiled. "I guess we have our Halloween costumes picked out."

"That's a couple of months away."

He didn't like how she averted her gaze. Did she think they wouldn't be together by then? "True, I don't know the game schedule off the top of my head." He played it off cool, like it didn't matter one way or the other. She was like a skittish doe watching and waiting with wide eyes to bolt at the slightest threat.

"Exactly, or where I'll be shooting a campaign."

"So will this hold you over until I get back?"

"No, but I bought heavy duty batteries for my vibrator."

Jake's cock hardened at the thought of watching the act. "Call me and I'll talk you through it." Why was he torturing himself?

There was that blush again. Even after what they just did he could still make her cheeks turn pink. It clutched at his heart. Despite her panic at the talk of the future, even if it only involved something as trivial as Halloween costumes, he reminded himself that she drove over three hours to jump him. His game plan was solid. Patience. And sex.

Jogging back to practice he tried to think of a good excuse for leaving the field but his mind was so filled with Hannah to care about the consequences. He hadn't gotten two feet onto the grass when the coach screamed. "Miller!"

Jake sprinted to the sideline. "What's up?"

"I hope it was worth 25 grand of that shiny new salary of yours."

Jake blinked as the coach's spit caught him in the eye as he continued to yell as if he were still across the field instead of right in front of him. Worth every damn penny to know Hannah missed him, hell it was damn priceless. But he couldn't say that to the coach who would up the fine to 50k. "Sorry, coach."

"Oh, your ass will be real sorry. After practice. Dead man runs along with your buddy Terell."

Still worth it as far as he was concerned, but what the hell did Terell do to piss off the coach?

After the fifth lap, Jake was vomiting over the bench and questioning his intelligence. He couldn't blame the summer heat, or the exhaustion from practice, and no, not even sex for the retched way he felt at this moment. He should've been able to stop his orgasm, but how could he resist losing himself inside her. Truthfully, he didn't know if it was possible to withhold anything from Hannah, but Heaven held a price.

Ryan jogged over to him. "Don't think that's going to get you off the hook."

"Shut up, Terell."

The coach bellowed across the field. "That's it for today, pussies."

"I'm getting too old for this shit," said Ryan. He sat down on the bench and handed Jake a towel.

"Thanks." Jake cleaned off and tossed the towel in the garbage. Looking up into the stands he hoped Hannah hadn't witnessed a weak moment. Relieved to find her attention elsewhere he still complained to Ryan, "I think she's signed more autographs today than the whole team combined."

"Oh, boo-hoo, the trials and tribulations of dating a supermodel."

"Hey, you're the one who got married."

"And you might as well be," fired back Ryan.

Despite the denial on his lips, Jake chewed on that for a moment and found that he would be lying if he did so instead he said, "Piss off."

Ryan laughed and grabbed his shoulder. "Hey, it happens to the best of us."

Jake shrugged it off. He looked back to Hannah now hoping to catch her attention. Did she get the same third degree from Samantha? If so, what sort of response did she give? "Oh crap," said Jake.

"What?"

"It's that piece of shit reporter." Even the wiliest of veteran players had gotten caught in the crosshairs of Ender's mean spirited column. The guy called himself a journalist but he was just a hack with an agenda to bring down the mightiest of players. No one was safe.

Ryan got up. "I wouldn't worry. It's not like Hannah is a stranger to the paparazzi."

"He's a slime. See you back at the rooms." Jake headed for the stands.

Ryan followed. "Oh no. Someone has to make sure you don't kill him."

As Hannah signed the last autograph a man who'd been hanging back approached her. Instinctually she knew he wasn't a fan. She caught Samantha's glance and she mouthed, "Be careful."

Dressed in khakis and a black polo shirt, she guessed he was in his forties. The slicked back hair made his nose appear large, like one of those caricatured sketches.

"Hannah, you here to tuck Miller into bed?"

She schooled her facial features to look naive. A trick she learned from modeling. "Who's asking?"

"The name's Ender. I'm with Sports Daily."

Hannah shook her head. "Don't know it. I'm a Cosmo girl."

The man smiled as if he were about to score a scoop. "Some say Miller's MVP award was a fluke and he's not worth the twenty million he's getting next year."

"Oh, I'll leave you experts to speculate on that." Oh how she wanted to defend Jake but in this case Hannah wisely chose to play dumb. This guy was a snake and from the look on Samantha's face she wanted to skin him alive. She wasn't the only one, but though Hannah knew zip about football, she knew how to play the media game.

"So it doesn't bother you if the media rakes him over the coals or if the fans boo him."

"Honey, I'm not with him for his skills on the football field." Hannah threw him off with her sweetest of smiles, but it was Jake's laughter that knocked her for a loop. She turned to see him standing two feet away ready to pounce if need be. Apparently he thought he had to protect her from the big bad reporter.

"And what skills would those be?" probed Ender.

"Why his cooking skills, of course," she said with such innocence she almost believed it. Hannah shook her head and left the reporter with a 'deer in the headlights' look on his face. She took Jake's arm and led him back down onto the field before any trouble started.

Chapter 11

J ake hummed as he packed his bag. He couldn't be happier about training camp ending. In three hours he'd be home ravishing Hannah for the following twenty-four hours until she had to leave for a week on an overseas assignment. Navigating his upcoming season with her erratic schedule would be a balancing act, but they'd make it work.

Ryan entered the room and held out his iPad. "Here, you might want to see this."

Jake took the sleek tablet from Ryan, the screen opened to the headline, 'Hannah Hahn Plays Jake Miller'.

Jake loosened his grip on the machine before he broke it in two. He didn't care about Ender's thoughts on Jake being led by his balls or that he wasn't worth a payday of twenty million a year. Stuff like that rolled off of him like dirt and sweat in the shower.

What Ender's interview with Hannah's mother revealed was another story. A photo of the woman accompanied the article. She may have been a beauty once but too much make-up and plastic surgery left her looking like a manne-quin.

"Samantha got a call from someone she knows at Sports Daily and he alerted her to Ender's vendetta. It's such crap and inflammatory that his paper wouldn't print it. So he sold it to them."

Jake nodded, noting the logo of one of the national gossip magazines. Ender had a lot nerve claiming Hannah was a fame seeker. The notoriety and money he got for this story put him in the same league. According to the mother, Hannah dated Jake only because he was the Super Bowl MVP and would do anything to be in the papers. Anything.

"My daughter couldn't possibly be serious over a half-breed like him."

Blooded rushed to the vein in his temple. As he read on each word pounded inside his head. The report alluded to rumors of Hannah posing nude before getting her big break.

Ryan paced the room. "The team will revoke his press credentials for this."

And they would. It was one thing for reporter to write a scathing column about a player's conduct on or off the field, quite another to print gossip and conjecture about a loved one.

Ryan added, "It's not true. None of it. But we didn't want you to be blindsided."

"Thanks Bro." Jake handed back the iPad with a non-chalance that covered up the doubt pricking inside his mind. Was she like every other female who would do anything for fame? No, he she wasn't with him for the publicity. Pissing off her mother seemed a more likely reason and it wouldn't be the first time Jake was used in such a way, but that happened in his teens.

"You okay?"

"Sure. Like you said—the trials and tribulations of dating a supermodel." Not since he'd been an adult had a female had the upper hand on him. Except for Hannah who held all the cards. When he got home he'd make sure they were laid out on the table.

His cell rang with Hannah's ring tone. He wouldn't jump to conclusions, if anything she was in it for the hot sex. That he DID know. But the nude pictures? "Hi, beautiful."

"Jake, did you see it?"

The sound of her tears only made him want to risk a dozen speeding tickets so he could be there to comfort her. "Don't worry, baby," his voice soothed. "I'll be home by five. We'll talk then. Okay?"

"I'm so sorry you're getting dragged into my family drama."

"We'll figure it out." The call ended and Jake had a long three-hour ride home to do just that.

Hannah greeted him at the door with a solemn hug. "I missed you."

Jake kissed her forehead. "I missed you, too" Walking into the living room, Jake dropped his bag to the floor. "Look Hannah, forget the article. It's apparent that we'll be the tabloids favorite targets for a while. We'll have to do our best not to feed into it." He paused, wishing it were that simple but there was one thing that needed to be settled. "I have to ask. At some point is there going to be pictures of you all over the Internet? Nude pictures?"

Hannah sat down on the couch. "There is a possibility yes, but if someone were to click on those images they would be arrested for child pornography."

"What?" His mind reeled.

"I understand if you want to leave me," she said, her voice weak with despair.

Rage burned in his blood. "The only place I'm going is to jail after I murder the perverted bastard who did that to you. Where the hell was your mother?"

"My mother?" Hannah's laughed chilled him to the bone. "She makes those moms of that toddler pageant show look like candidates for Mothers of the Year. I was home schooled but all I knew were manicures and spray tans from the time I was two. I wasn't raised—I was groomed like a fucking show pony!"

"Hannah, no—"

"She ordered me to do it and when I refused she took what little I had on, off. I was fifteen."

Jake tried to process this. How can someone who is supposed to love you treat you like you were nothing? How did someone recover from something like that? *You don't.* The physicals scars his father inflicted were nothing compared to the emotional ones he still carried.

"You know how twisted I am? I thought doing Playboy would exercise the demons because this time I would be in control. And then you said no and it made me feel dirty all over again which is why I broke it off and never returned your calls."

Stunned by the realization, Jake knelt at her feet and said, "I didn't know. I would never make you feel bad about yourself."

"I know. You've been nothing but good to me."

His hand cupped her cheek. "I was falling for you and the thought of other men seeing you naked drove me insane," he confessed.

"You were falling for me? What about now?"

Her eyes wide with innocence tugged at his protective instincts. "I'm still in the midst of the fall and I've been reaching to grab onto to something, anything, to make sense of it all."

"Maybe if we held onto each other?" Both her hands came to rest upon his shoulders.

Her blossoming trust in him caused his heart to thud like booms of thunder. "I think that's a great idea." That stunning smile sent him reeling. Lightning struck deep within in his chest, his fall complete. But he couldn't tell her now, didn't want the purity of what he was feeling to be linked to the sad admission of her past. She'd probably think he said it out of pity. No, he'd hold onto the words for now, until she was ready to hear them, until she was ready to say them back.

Chapter 12

Hannah lounged in her agent's corner office. She was about to sign a lucrative contract that would make her the spokeswoman for a new cosmetics line. Like the world needed another one. She glanced at her watch. What was she doing here? She didn't need another gig or the money that came with it.

Between Jake's football games and her modeling assignments that had been taking her to the four corners of the world they'd been the proverbial ships passing in the night. Perhaps that was a good thing and why their three-month anniversary approached. For Hannah it was a milestone she had never reached.

Jake's bye week was coming up and she left her schedule free so they could enjoy it together, but with her stomach still roiling with the effects of a horrendous flu bug she caught while in Nepal she didn't hold out much hope.

Francine dressed in a sophisticated white Chanel suit and sporting a pair of fake eyeglasses entered the room. Her hair looked like spun silver and Hannah imagined that one day her blonde locks would turn the same shade.

Francine didn't bother to sit down. "I'm sorry, you didn't get it."

One part of Hannah nearly slouched in relief, but a model never slouches unless you're contorting your body into a high fashion pose. Another part, however, balked at the snub. "Who did?"

"Lily. And from what I hear for half your going rate."

Fresh faced and young, Lily was a rising star in the fashion world. While Hannah was old news, a fading star destined to fall. Hannah laughed at the drama of her own making. Couldn't blame a company for saving money. There'd be other campaigns she told herself, but her mother's voice drowned out reason and replaced it with doubt.

"You've been working too hard. Take a break. Go to the spa," advised Francine.

"Is spa code for 'get a little work done'?"

"No! Forget them. Start your own cosmetics line."

"Or a clothing line," ventured Hannah.

"Yes! That wedding gown you designed for your friend has been copied by hundreds of brides."

Hannah rose and thanked Francine, agreeing that she needed some time off. Her agent began to speak, but stopped.

"What?"

Francine's gaze swept in Hannah's body, "Is there any possibility you might be pregnant?"

"No way." Her response was automatic but as she headed for the elevator her thoughts zeroed in on the one time Jake didn't use a condom. The grave voice of her tenth grade Health teacher sounded in her mind, 'All it takes is one time.' But she hadn't had her period months prior to that. *And haven't since then either.*

She stopped walking and placed a hand on her belly. *Could I be?*

As she left the building, Brianna, a model represented by the same agency, ran up to her. "Hannah, darling, so sorry to hear you lost out."

"First time for everything." In this business bad news travels faster than the speed of sound.

"That's how it starts. Everybody wants you when you're hot, and well, you look a little worn out. Here's the name of my plastic surgeon. He practices out of the Cayman Islands and is very discreet. My bookings have doubled since I've gotten back." Brianna slid the business card into Hannah's hand as if she were passing an illegal drug.

Did she really need work done? Hannah always thought she'd age gracefully, but faced with the harsh reality of her business she began to consider it.

She threw the card into her purse and flagged a cab. Settled in the backseat she fished out her compact and lipstick. The cab jolted sending a red line across her face. Cursing, she grabbed a tissue, wetted it with her mouth and tried to rub the mark away. The reflection staring back looked like an escapee from a clown college or worse like a used whore. Scrambling for another tissue her hand touched the business card and she reluctantly pulled it out. Brianna did look amazing and she was a year older than Hannah.

Maybe this is just what she needed. A little pick me up. She placed all the items back in her purse and called the number. No way she was pregnant. A week in the Cayman

Islands and she'd come back looking and feeling brand new.

A few hours later she sat fidgeting in a chair across from Jake. While dining on his mother's spaghetti and meatballs, Jake mentioned her upcoming visit. As much as she wanted to meet the woman who raised such a wonderful man, Hannah didn't know the first thing about impressing Jake's mother. Here was a woman who flew into town just to pack up her son's freezer with home cooked meals, while Hannah didn't bake or sew or take care of Jake in any way. Except for the bedroom, of course.

"What's up?"

Hannah looked up to see Jake's concerned face. She'd been trying to figure out how to tell him about her trip without revealing the reason behind it. She took a deep breath. "I'm leaving for Cayman tomorrow."

"Tomorrow? But you're eating carbs."

The man knew her all too well. The lie was on her lips but she couldn't tell him it was a last minute assignment. If she expected him to share what was going on in his life then he deserved the same. Besides he'd notice the change when she got back. "I'm having a little work done."

"The hell you are!"

His fist fell upon the table causing the silverware to jump along with Hannah's nerves. She gathered herself together ready to fend off any resistance. "It's my body."

"No, it isn't. It belongs to the products you sell."

"Oh and you wouldn't get a surgery if it meant prolonging your playing days?"

"That's different."

"How?" Hannah stood, her arms at her sides and her hands fisted looking down at Jake.

"Because it's exactly what your mother would tell you to do."

"Oh that is low!" Hannah turned away, tears welling up in her eyes.

"It's the truth. She's may be physically out of your life, but she's residing inside your head."

She spun around to face him, his words cutting up her insides. "What do you want from me?" she shouted.

The vein on his temple pulsed. "I want you to see yourself the way I see you," he yelled.

Startled, Hannah jumped back, but he took a deep breath and stood, stepping forward to hold her hand and gently said, "I want you to love yourself the way I love you."

He loved her? Looking into his eyes she caught a glimpse of what he saw. To him she was beautiful inside and out. And he loved her. Of course he did, who else would put up with her.

He, on the other hand, was so easy to love. "Oh, Jake, I, I—" Her hand flew up to her mouth, to keep the contents of her stomach from flying out and ran to the bathroom, reaching it just in time.

Jake followed her in. "Hannah, are you okay?"

"Go away," she moaned into the toilet. She didn't want him to see her this way. Was there anything worse to throw up than spaghetti? Her stomach heaved again. Maybe she was pregnant.

"Fine, I'll go."

"I didn't mean—" But it was too late. He was gone. And she didn't have the strength to go chase after him.

Crawling into bed, she called Samantha and asked her to stop at the pharmacy in the morning before coming over. Hannah couldn't walk into a drug store and buy a pregnancy test without it being reported on in every magazine in creation. After what felt like the Inquisition from Samantha, Hannah hung up the phone and fell into a fitful sleep.

Dreams flitted in and out. Then one so vivid she woke up in a whimper. Mommie Dearest made a guest appearance, mocking Hannah over and over again.

"I made you a star."

"It's Paris, it's okay here."

"There that wasn't so bad."

"He won't love you when you swell up like a hot air balloon."

It didn't matter she already lost him. And when she confirmed in the morning that she was pregnant he'd think it was a desperate attempt to win him back. She imagined Jake's strong body next to hers, even felt a shift of weight as if he were turning over.

"Feeling better?"

Did she dream that sexy deep voice? Opening her eyes she rolled into his open arms. "You didn't leave me." She clung to him as if she thought she was still dreaming and she'd wake to a nightmare of an empty bed.

"Leave you? I went to the store to buy you ginger ale and Nilla Wafers." He smoothed her hair back. "But by the time I got back you were already zonked out."

"I didn't mean go away as in for good." The panic in Hannah's voice remained, despite his reassuring words.

"Its okay, shhh. I realized that about a minute after walking out the door."

The words she held inside her heart but so afraid to voice flowed out in a breathless whisper, "I love you Jake."

"Wow. You didn't throw up. Progress."

Hannah laughed. "Sorry about that."

"Will you promise me something?"

"I'm not doing it."

Jake's skeptic look made her laugh again.

"I promise."

His fingers caressed her cheek. "Your beautiful, Hannah. Maybe I don't tell you enough."

"You make me feel beautiful."

His smile lit her heart afire – and other places too. "I'm feeling much better."

Hannah rushed to get dressed. Samantha would be there in less than ten minutes with the pregnancy test and her screaming bladder counted every second. Deciding to pace in the living room, she walked out to find Jake still in the apartment. "Aren't you supposed to be at practice?"

"Good morning to you too."

"I'm sorry, you startled me."

"How are you feeling?"

"Okay." The doorbell rang and she rushed to answer it, ignoring Jake's question of who she was expecting.

Hannah opened the door and pulled Samantha inside. "He's still here," she said in a tight whisper. "Act natural." But they did anything but as they rushed by Jake with fake smiles on their way to the bathroom.

Closing the door, Hannah grabbed the bag from Samantha, ripped it open along with the packaging. She didn't know which was worse—the anticipation of the results or the urgency to pee. Once she squatted over the toilet she had to ask Samantha to turn around. Done, Hannah calmly laid the stick down on the back of the toilet and washed her hands. "Are you timing it?"

Samantha nodded and began waving her hand like the motion would make time go faster. The two minutes seemed to stretch into eternity, but when Samantha said okay, Hannah stood frozen unable to move. The result would change everything.

'If you don't look, I will."

She slapped Samantha's hand as she went to reach for the stick. Hannah bent forward to read the results.

"Well, what does it say?" prodded Samantha.

In shock, Hannah straightened. "I'm pregnant," she said simply.

"And are we happy about this?" Samantha's look of anticipation was filled with hope.

Hannah paused. Truthfully, she never pictured herself with children, but she'd never pictured herself loving a man either. Would she be a good mother? She didn't know, but she would try with all her heart to be one. At least she knew not what to do. "Yes. I'm scared out of my mind," she admitted, but then started to giggle as euphoria replaced fear, "Yes, yes I'm happy."

Samantha screamed, sharing in the joy, and Hannah joined in as they both jumped up and down. The celebration subsided and she realized something still scared her. "How do I tell Jake?"

Jake risked his second fine of the season by ditching the morning practice, but though he believed Hannah last night about the plastic surgery he didn't trust that she'd feel the same way in the morning. He figured he'd wait around to see how she was feeling.

He approached the bathroom hoping to ease drop. The sudden shouts from behind the door surprised him and he backed away to the living room fitting the pieces together. The crinkled up bag and Samantha's sly smile when she passed by him on the mad dash to the bathroom.

Samantha was pregnant.

Ryan was going to be one happy man. Jake wondered if Hannah would catch the baby bug. She was so obsessed with having the perfect body would she risk what it would do to her figure?

The door opened and the two of them stepped out into the living room, giggling.

"Congratulations Samantha."

"Oh no, no, the congratulations aren't mine," she blurted. "Oh, I better go." She mouthed 'Call me' to Hannah.

He re-organized the facts and the pieces thunder into place, the bag, the screaming, Hannah's ongoing vomiting – morning sickness. "You're pregnant?"

"Wow, that was easy. I'm so glad you're a smart man and figured out..."

As she rambled on so did the thoughts in his mind. How? When? She said she was safe. But none of that mattered. Hannah was pregnant. With his baby. And she was happy about it.

So was he. Shocked, but happy. He tried to speak, but with the way she was going on and on, he didn't think he'd be able to get in a word.

"... I hadn't had my period in months when we—"

Jake did what any man would do and pulled her into a kiss. Already breathless, she greedily sucked in the air he breathed in to her until he was the one needing oxygen. Which was fine with him. He'd give her the air he breathed, his heart, his soul. He'd give her the family she'd never had. He'd give her everything because that's what she meant to him. Everything.

Chapter 13

At eight months and two weeks, Hannah's supermodel runaway walk was reduced to a waddle. Still naked from the shower, she reached for the cream to rub over her swelled stomach hoping to prevent stretch marks.

Jake entered the bedroom with a bag of Godiva truffles. "Hey, beautiful. Let me do that." He threw the bag onto the bed as he reached for the jar.

Any worries that he wouldn't feel the same way when she grew fat faded long ago. In fact, he seemed to love her even more. Probably due to some male genetic pride passed down from the cavemen. But she came to love her body; even if it came after months of therapy. Still, her personal trainer was on speed dial as soon as the doctor gave the okay to resume exercising.

Jake knelt at her feet and kissed her rounded belly. In turn she stroked his bald head smiling at the picture they must make. The tabloids would pay a fortune for the shot, but this moment was for them alone, to be remembered inside her heart for the rest of her life.

Lovingly smoothing on the cream, Jake hummed a tune. Hannah's mouth dropped opened and she dragged in a breath. The baby kicked like she was auditioning for the Radio City Rockettes.

"Whoa!" Jake met her gaze, his smile wide with amazement.

"It's a girl, for sure."

"You think so?"

"Every time she hears her Daddy's voice she performs a Salsa inside me."

"A girl? Hmmm." Jake resumed his humming.

Jake made her believe in happy ever after. He'd asked her numerous times to marry. Samantha, Ryan and what seemed like the whole wide world had been after her to marry. But it wasn't the outside world pressuring her that changed her mind but the weight of the baby she carried with such love that she didn't know it was possible. And Jake shared that love with her. "I think it sounds good. Don't you? Maxine Miller?"

Jake stood. A silly smile on his face and eyes filled with surprise. "Does that mean you'll marry me?"

"Yes. Not that you've asked me in a whole week." Hannah pretended to be offended.

"I was saving the 100th proposal for the delivery room."

Hannah laughed. It wasn't quite a hundred. "You didn't even notice that I re-decorated the bedroom." Samantha called it nesting, but now seeped in whites and blacks, the décor reflected the taste of a modern, sophisticated couple. She kept the chandelier though, after all a girl needed a little bling in the bedroom.

Jake looked about the room. "It's nice, but all I need is a bed to make love to you in." He leaned in to kiss her, but she grabbed his arm in a death grip as a contraction hit.

"It's time."

He eased her onto the bed. "Two weeks early? It can't be a girl," he joked.

"I am NOT amused." Hannah winced at her tone. She swore she wouldn't be a bitch in the delivery room, wouldn't be one of those frantic women who yelled awful things. "Sorry."

Jake chuckled. "Save them all for the end, otherwise you're going to wear yourself out."

Now that was funny and she laughed herself right into another contraction. When it passed he helped her dress in the designated outfit for the ride to the hospital—a simple sweat suit. Oh how the mighty have fallen. Finished he said, "It's more fun taking your clothes off."

Hannah giggled again. "Will you stop, I'm going to pop the baby right here!"

Panic lit up his eyes. Jake grabbed the packed bag from the closet. "All set?"

"Yep." They rushed out the door, but Hannah stopped as they reached the elevators saying, "Wait!"

Eyes filled with concern, Jake asked, "Another contraction? So soon?"

"No. You forgot the truffles!"

Hannah laughed as Jake dashed back into the apartment as if he were running down the field for a touchdown. How deep could her love go for this man?

He returned with the bag. "Your wish is my command."

With Jake at her side there was nothing left to wish for. She had it all.

Six hours and an empty bag of truffles later, Maxine Lee Miller was born into the world.

About the Author

Liz Matis is a mild-mannered accountant by day and romance writer by night. She believes in happily ever after.

Please visit her blog at: www.taoofliz.blogspot.com

Email: elizabethmatis@gmail.com

Twitter: @LizMatis

Facebook Like: www.facebook.com/pages/Liz-Matis-Fan-Page/308197599253896

Goodreads: www.goodreads.com/photo/author/5289185.Liz_Matis

Pinterest: www.pinterest.com/lizmatis/

Liz would like to thank Juan M. Frisanccio Muñoz for permitting the use of his poem.

Thank you for reading GOING FOR IT. If you enjoyed, please tell other readers why you liked this book by reviewing it at your favorite online retailer, as well as Goodreads.

AVAILABLE NOW:

Playing For Keeps – *Fantasty Football: Season 1*
by Liz Matis
(Samantha and Ryan's story)

Winner of the New England Romance Writers of America
First Kiss Contest

Journalist Samantha Jameson always wanted to be one of the boys, but Ryan Terell won't let her join the club. Fresh from the battlegrounds of Iraq, reporting on a bunch of overgrown boys playing pro football is just the change of scenery she needs. If trying to be taken seriously in the world of sports writing wasn't hard enough, Ryan, her college crush, is only making it harder. As a tight-end for the team she's covering, he is strictly off limits.

Ryan Terell is a playmaker on and off the field, but when Samantha uncovers his moves, he throws out the playbook. Just as he claims his sweetest victory, Samantha's investigation into a steroid scandal involving his team forces him to call a time-out to their off the record trysts. But then a life threatening injury on the field will force them both to decide just how far they'll go to win the game.

Love By Design
by Liz Matis

Design Intervention starts the second season with its own surprise makeover. Interior designer Victoria Bryce must break in her temporary co-host, Aussie Russ Rowland.

Victoria, former socialite wild child hopes the reality show will give her the clout to launch her own design line without her family connections. Russ, former bad boy Australian TV star is using the show to launch his acting career in the States.

Sparks fly on camera as they argue over paint colors and measurement mishaps leading to passions igniting behind the scenes. But when their pasts collide with the present will the foundation they built withstand the final reveal?

Real Men Don't Drink Appletinis
by Liz Matis
An eBook novelette

Hollywood's handsomest men surround celebrity agent Ava Gardner but none are as intriguing as larger-than-life Grady O'Flynn. The Navy SEAL is on an unsanctioned mission when they end up starring in their own romantic comedy.

Will they continue to sizzle when Grady has to report back to duty? In this sexy novelette by Liz Matis, two lovers have two weeks to find out.